## "Hey, you okay?" Chief Morgan Wright asked, kneeling beside the woman.

His instincts piqued when the other female whipped around the corner and raced for the opposite end of the ferry. They went on red alert when he spotted a strange man make that same turn and start searching between cars.

"Ma'am?" he asked again. She didn't answer at first. He'd seen her go down, flat on her stomach.

"Don't hurt me," she gasped.

"You're okay. I'm a police officer."

She sat up and the air ripped from his chest. No, it couldn't be. He'd never forget the face of his first love. Julie Burns, the girl who'd taken a piece of his heart with her when she'd left ten years ago.

An eternal optimist, **Hope White** was born and raised in the Midwest. She and her college sweetheart have been married for thirty years and are blessed with two wonderful sons, two feisty cats and a bossy border collie. When not dreaming up inspirational tales, Hope enjoys hiking, sipping tea with friends and going to the movies. She loves to hear from readers, who can contact her at hopewhiteauthor@gmail.com.

# CHRISTMAS HAVEN

## HOPE WHITE

**❖ HARLEQUIN**® LOVE INSPIRED® SUSPENSE

Recycling programs
for this product may
not exist in your area.

 LOVE INSPIRED BOOKS

ISBN-13: 978-0-373-80375-0

Christmas Haven

www.Harlequin.com

Printed in U.S.A.

Do not judge, and you will not be judged.
Do not condemn, and you will not be condemned.
Forgive, and you will be forgiven.
*—Luke* 6:37

To Drex—Dream a little dream, my friend.

# Chapter One

Julie Burns had planned to visit her family for Christmas, but not like this, not running from danger.

She dug her fingernails into the strap of her backpack and quickened her step. Heart pounding in her chest, she crossed Sunset, eyeing the ferry terminal ahead.

She was close, a block away from hopping the ferry and escaping the threat.

She hoped.

"Don't be paranoid," she told herself as she shot a quick glance over her shoulder.

The last thing she wanted was to draw attention by acting nervous. She'd tucked her blond hair into a knit hat, put on her glasses, which she rarely wore, and hopped the bus to the Edmonds Ferry Terminal from downtown. She did everything she could to look average, nondescript. Invisible.

The police hadn't been able to help her. Not when she'd reported Andy missing, or when she reported the kidnapping of Dane Simms, another teenage street kid that she worked with at Teen Life. When Julie's office had been broken into, the cops had investigated, but chalked it up to a random burglary. She sensed there was more to it.

Then she started getting anonymous calls and felt as if someone was watching her, waiting for an opportunity to…

Out of the corner of her eye, she spotted a dark sedan cruising slowly past. She focused on the doors to the ferry terminal, closing in, nearly there.

"Excuse me?" a man called out from the car.

She ignored him at first, hoping he was speaking to someone else.

"Miss? Is this the ferry to Kingston?"

*Breathe. It's okay. He's just asking a question.*

She turned to the driver, a clean-cut-looking man in his thirties. "Yes, it is."

"Great. Do you know where they line up? It's my first time on a ferry."

"I think back on the main street, there." She pointed.

"Thanks very much." He smiled and pulled away to get in line.

With a slight shake of her head, she refocused on buying her ticket. *Relax, don't be so paranoid.* She'd taken precautions to make sure no one had followed her and had removed all her personal information from files at work, which wasn't easy with Helen spying over her shoulder. The woman was always looking for an opportunity to point out Julie's shortcomings to their boss. She'd probably lead the rally to fire Julie when she didn't show up for work tomorrow.

Julie couldn't worry about office drama. She'd packed a bag this morning so she wouldn't have to go back to her apartment after her dinner meeting, and instead came straight to the ferry terminal.

To escape, back to her hometown of Port Whisper. Morgan's smile flashed across her thoughts and regret sliced through her chest. It surprised her. She didn't think it would still hurt. Not after all this time.

But Morgan Wright had been her first true love.

Her only true love.

Now, with her work schedule counseling homeless teens, she had little time for romance, but didn't miss it. She wondered if that was because she'd had her chance at love with Morgan and blew it.

"Don't think about it," she hushed.

It only added to her anxiety. To calm herself, she pictured her hometown, the safe, predictable, boring world in which she'd grown up.

And had left ten years ago. She'd had to leave. She'd needed to do more by helping underprivileged teens in Seattle.

It had seemed like a good plan, until last week, when it all fell apart.

She bought her ticket and headed up the ramp to board the ferry.

Heading home. Something she said she'd never do. Not because it was a bad place, but she couldn't bring herself to go back and be that person again, a small-town girl living in a city where the biggest crisis was the Langford brothers breaking into Stuckey's Hardware to steal supplies to make pipe bombs.

The teens she counseled dealt with homelessness and drug use, abusive parents and a bleak future. She wanted to help the people who really needed her.

She shifted into a booth by the window and pulled out her phone, feeling bad for having to abandon her team. They'd had no idea about her plans to leave when she'd smiled across the dinner table at them tonight. But there were no other options. She sensed the danger trailing her and had to get away. She figured the less they knew about her plans the safer they'd be.

Thinking of how she'd craft *that* email to her boss, Andrea, she noticed a text message alert. She clicked on it and the message opened:

I see you.

She gasped and whipped her head around, eyeing the passengers in the immediate area: a group of kids with a parent; a hippie-looking guy curled up and asleep on the bench; a mom with two kids, one in a stroller.

Should she get off the ferry and wait for the next one? Notify ferry personnel?

And say what? That she feared she was being stalked but couldn't be sure?

She continued scanning other passengers as the ferry started across the water: a businessman in suit and tie, working on his laptop; a threesome of middle-aged folks laughing as one told a story.

Walking toward her was the man who'd asked for directions to the ferry line. He eyed his phone, stopped dead in his tracks and looked right at her. He smiled. Goose bumps pricked down her arms.

She got up and headed for the snack bar, bustling with passengers anxious to fill their stomachs. *Look relaxed, casual. You don't know he was the one who sent the text.*

She wandered up to a pack of teenagers who eyed foil-wrapped burgers. The thought of food made her stomach twist into a tighter knot. The hair bristled on the back of her neck, instinct warning her to get away.

She grabbed a sandwich and lined up to check out. Glancing over her shoulder, she spotted the car guy in line a few people behind her.

"Seven eighty-seven," the cashier said.

Julie fumbled in her pocket for cash. Her fingers trembled as she desperately strategized her next move. She handed the cashier a ten and took off, rushing toward the stairs, hoping to hide between the cars below.

Would he jump the line and follow her? She couldn't think about that, she had to get away, had to—

She raced down the stairs and flung open the door. Rushing up the aisle, she used the cars as cover, ducking between them so as not to be seen. She crisscrossed the ferry and glanced over her shoulder. A tall figure headed toward her.

She stumbled on something and went down, dropping her sandwich and slamming her palms to the ground to brace her fall. But it was too late. She was down and he was close. She could feel his eyes boring into her back.

And saw a shadow loom above her.

"Hey, you okay?" Morgan Wright asked, kneeling beside the frantic woman.

His instincts piqued when she dodged around the corner and raced for the opposite end of the ferry as if she was a sprinter in the Olympics. They went on red alert when he spotted a tall male make the same turn and search between cars.

"Ma'am?" he tried again. She didn't answer at first. He'd seen her hit the ground and figured she was out of breath.

"Don't hurt me," she gasped.

"You're okay," he assured. "I'm a police officer."

She sat up and the air ripped from his chest. No, it couldn't be. He'd never forget the face of his first love, never forget her golden eyes or freckles that dotted her nose.

He'd never forgotten Julie Burns, the girl who'd taken a piece of his heart with her when she'd left ten years ago.

Lower lip trembling, she clutched her wrist to her stomach, rocking forward slightly. She still hadn't looked at him.

A tornado of emotions whipped through his

body, from anger to pain to concern. And he had so many questions.

"I… He was…" she choked.

"Take a deep breath," Morgan said, touching her shoulder for support. That's what he'd do if she were a stranger. He decided that was the best way to keep his perspective.

To treat her as if she were a stranger.

He spotted movement out of the corner of his eye. A tall man, thirties, with slicked-back hair, wearing an overcoat, froze ten feet away. Was it the man who'd been searching between cars? Morgan couldn't be sure.

"Can I help you?" Morgan stood to his full six feet two inches.

"She forgot her change upstairs." He hesitated and extended his hand to reveal a few bills and coins.

Morgan reached for it.

"Who are you?" The guy closed his fist.

"A cop." He flashed his badge. "I'll take it from here."

The guy dropped the money into Morgan's hand and eyed Julie. "Is she okay?"

"She tripped. She'll be fine." Morgan glanced at Julie, who still hadn't looked up, then back at the stranger. "You a friend of hers?"

The guy backed off. "No, I just happened to be in line behind her."

Uh-huh. Right.

"Good Samaritan type," Morgan said. "Thought we'd lost all of those. Thanks again," he said in dismissal.

With a nod the guy disappeared into the stairwell.

Morgan took a deep breath and kneeled beside Julie. She was white as a sheet, dazed and looked as if she was going into shock.

"Jules, hey, it's really okay."

She blinked, the sound of her nickname snapping her out of the trance. Glancing at Morgan, she gasped.

"Morgan…" She closed her eyes. "I'm dead, right? I'm dead and went to heaven."

Interesting that she thought seeing Morgan equaled heaven.

"You're not dead. Just shaken up."

She eyed him, a tear trailing down her cheek.

He remembered the last time he'd seen her cry. He thought they were happy tears, but they'd been tears of goodbye.

"I don't understand," she said.

"To see me in heaven I'd have to be dead and I'm very much alive, which means you're very much alive." He sounded like a dork, but finding the right words, any intelligent words, at this point was a challenge.

He was on the ferry headed back home. With Julie.

A scene that had filled his dreams more than once in the years after she'd left.

Shifting into police mode he asked, "Do you want to tell me what happened?"

"I fell."

"I gathered as much."

She tipped her head slightly, a habit he'd found endearing years ago.

"Why are you on the ferry?" she asked.

"Coming home from seeing my dad in the hospital. Why are you on the ferry?"

"Mom needs help."

Short sentences seemed to be all she could utter. He guessed the trauma still buzzed in her system.

"Huh, news to me," he said. "I saw her yesterday and she looked fine."

"Housecleaning."

Now he knew she was half in shock. Edith Burns kept a tidy house, was the most organized person Morgan knew and baked a mean pecan-chocolate pie.

"Housecleaning?" he prodded.

She gave him a quick nod, looking like a little girl.

*Don't do it, Morgan. Don't get sucked in.*

"Did she send you to get me?" she asked.

She was up to seven-word sentences. That had to be a good thing, right?

"No, she didn't send me. Take your hat off," he said, changing the subject. He didn't like seeing her like this, frightened and disoriented.

"What? Why?" she asked.

"I need to check for a head wound."

She absently slipped the knit cap from her head and golden strands of sunlight fell across her shoulders. Clenching his jaw, he ran his hand gently across her scalp looking for a contusion. He struggled to ignore the feel of the soft-spun gold against his fingertips.

"I didn't hit my head. I don't think," she said.

He removed his hands and leaned back on his heels. "Nope, doesn't look like it. You wanna tell me what got you so spooked?"

"I—" her breath caught. "I was…" Her voice trailed off and she clasped her hands in her lap, he guessed to keep them from trembling.

Morgan touched her shoulder once again, hoping to ground her. "Come on."

Gripping her upper arm, he coaxed her up. He'd forgotten how perfectly matched they were with her five-foot-eight-inch height to Morgan's six foot two. She'd been teased in grade school for being a giant, but the teasing stopped when she turned into a beautiful teenage girl.

His girl.

"I can't believe I tripped," she said, avoiding his gaze.

He could. She was terrified, and eventually she was going to tell him why. But not now. Now he had to help her calm down.

Cupping her elbow, he guided her to his truck.

"I'm such a klutz," she offered.

She was anything but a klutz. She'd been a star athlete at Greenwood High, center on the basketball team, track star, and she had looked breathtaking in a prom dress.

This was bad, very bad. He needed to take her to her mom's and get as far away as possible from this woman. And his past.

He opened the truck door. She took off her backpack and climbed into the front seat. It suddenly hit him how surreal this was. Running into Julie on the ferry? Rescuing her?

Morgan glanced over his shoulder to see if the guy who'd brought her change was anywhere in the vicinity. A Good Samaritan? Perhaps. Yet the guy looked as if he'd been caught stealing when Morgan noticed him.

Morgan slid behind the wheel of his truck and locked the doors. They couldn't dock fast enough. At least when he was driving he'd have to concentrate on the dark roads leading to Port Whisper. But sitting here on the ferry… he dreaded the awkward conversation.

"How have you been?" she asked.

"Good. You?" He didn't look at her, fearing the resentment would rise up this throat against his will.

"Okay, I guess."

Just okay? She'd fled Port Whisper, ran away from Morgan to save the world. She'd sacrificed true love and she was *just* okay?

*Knock it off.*

"I work with street kids," she offered.

"Sounds like a worthy endeavor."

"It is. It's…fulfilling."

Unlike staying in her hometown, marrying Morgan and raising a family.

*Ancient history.*

He thought he'd moved on. He'd been engaged once, thought he'd found love again. But Renee couldn't turn down an offer to teach in the Midwest, and Morgan wouldn't abandon his dad.

Sure, he'd recovered from Renee's heartbreak, occasionally dating Anna, another hometown girl.

But she wasn't Julie.

Unbelievable. Why did they have to be on the same boat?

"You said your dad was in the hospital," Julie said. "What's wrong?"

"Cancer."

"I'm sorry." She leaned back against the headrest and sighed.

Seconds stretched like hours between them. Fine. Silence was better than talking about their past.

Her cell vibrated and she pulled it out. "Hey, Mom. Yeah...okay. You'll never believe who I ran into on the ferry. Morgan Wright." She glanced at him and smiled.

He ripped his gaze from hers and focused on the Camry in front of them. It was dangerous to look too long at that gentle smile, the whir of emotions building in his chest.

"I don't know, hang on." She glanced at Morgan.

"Can you give me a ride to my mom's?"

"Absolutely." Great, now *he* was down to one-word sentences. Shock did that to a person, and he was still in shock after running into her tonight.

"Sure, Mom, he'll drop me off. Okay, I'll tell him. Love you, too."

She pocketed her phone and glanced at Morgan. "She wants you to come in and say hi."

"Can't tonight."

Or tomorrow. Or ever.

The Burnses' house brought back too many memories. It had been a safe place, a nurturing place for Morgan to hide out when his dad was in one of his moods. He'd had a lot of those after Morgan's mom left.

Morgan never understood how Julie could have traded such a safe, loving home for the threat of working with street kids. He'd kept up with her life through the town grapevine, not intentionally, of course, but the news always made its way to him through one source or another: Did you hear that Julie got her master's degree? Julie was honored by the city of Seattle? Julie is saving runaway teenagers?

"So, I heard you went into the family business," she said.

"Yep. I'm police chief."

"How are things in Port Whisper?" she asked.

"Busy. Developers have discovered us. A new resort is under construction. Don't you talk to your sister?"

"I do," she said defensively.

"Seems like her snack shop and tourist business has picked up."

"Never pegged Lana for a tour guide in a small town."

"Right, it's not as exciting as saving street kids," he let slip.

She pinned him with her golden eyes. "What I meant was, she was always so shy."

"How long will you be in Port Whisper?" He hoped not long.

"Not sure. Depends on how long it takes to help Mom."

He'd managed to avoid Julie the other times she'd visited. He'd thrown himself into a home-improvement project at Dad's, or taken a few days off to go fishing with the guys, anything but come face-to-face with heartbreak. He'd been a fool to think she'd choose Morgan over her career. But back then he was young and hopeful.

*Buddy, you have so not gotten over this woman.*

"I feel like we need to talk about something," she started.

"What's that?"

"You know."

He glanced at her, casual, aloof. "No, I really don't." He hesitated. "Oh, you mean why you were terrified a few minutes ago?"

With a disappointed frown, she glanced out the passenger window to study the side-view mirror.

"Did you know that guy?" he pressed.

"No. He was just a guy I gave directions to."

"Which is why you were freaked when you rushed around the corner?"

She rested her forehead against the window and closed her eyes, indicating the conversation was over.

Good. He'd successfully avoided the gut-wrenching subject of their failed relationship. Why did she want to go there, anyway?

He clicked on the radio to a country station. A song about lost love and regret filled the car. He punched the radio off.

During his tour in Iraq he'd faced off against insurgents, been shot at and nearly blown up a handful of times. But nothing made him feel as threatened as sitting next to Jules.

For some reason, being near her exposed his vulnerability like nothing else could. He felt as if he was going into battle without a flak jacket, weapons or common sense.

And he didn't believe in coincidences.

*What's the message, Lord? What am I supposed to do with this situation?*

He wished he could trust his heart to guide him.

Unfortunately, the woman sitting inches away had destroyed his heart. That's probably why he couldn't get close to Anna, and why he used his charming smile and jokes to keep people at a distance. He never let anyone inside. It wasn't worth the risk.

Maybe running into Julie was his final test, his last challenge before being able to move on.

And he was so ready to move on.

# Chapter Two

*The warmth of Morgan's hand holding hers shot a sense of peace across her body as they lay in the grass overlooking Puget Sound. She closed her eyes, savoring this moment, wanting it to last forever.*

*"Are you cold?" he asked.*

*She turned to look into his blue-green eyes, filled with love and adoration.*

*"No, I'm perfect," she whispered.*

*"That you are." He leaned over and kissed her, his lips soft and gentle. Her heart tapped against her chest.*

Love. This is what love feels like, *she thought.* She wanted to hang on to it. Forever.

*Then it was gone, her lips suddenly chilled, her hands frigid.*

*She opened her eyes to an empty spot where Morgan had just been beside her.*

*"Morgan?"*

*A gunshot echoed across the water. She jumped to her feet and spun around to see Morgan fall to his knees, clutching his chest.*

*"Morgan!"*

*She rushed to him, gripping his shoulders, searching his eyes. They were coal black, dead. He fell to the ground, blood staining his shirt.*

*"No!" A sob racked her chest.*

*"Yes," a voice said. Through tear-filled eyes she glanced up, struggling to focus on the man standing a few feet away.*

*"And now it's your turn."*

*BANG!*

"No!" she screamed.

"Julie, wake up."

She couldn't breathe, couldn't see past the shooter's black eyes… Morgan's lifeless eyes. Heartbreak ripped through her.

"Jules." He pulled her against his chest. "Wake up."

A choke-sob escaped her lips as she clung to his leather jacket, willing the images away.

"It's okay. You're home," Morgan said.

Boy, did she feel home as she leaned into his solid chest and inhaled the scent of pine mixed with aftershave.

For a few seconds she basked in the feeling

of security...of love. Then the flash of Morgan being shot, the life dimming from his eyes and the blood covering his shirt, shot a new wave of panic through her body.

"I shouldn't have fallen asleep," she said, breaking the embrace and casting a worried glance out the back window. They were at her mom's.

"No one followed us," Morgan offered as if reading her mind.

She whipped the car door open and charged up the driveway, needing to get away from him. The front door swung open and Mom opened her arms. Julie welcomed the gesture and held on tight.

"Hey, what's all this?" her mom asked.

Julie couldn't form words past the terror of her nightmare.

Morgan had been killed. Because of her.

It had only been a dream, but it felt real. She wouldn't be responsible for the death of someone she cared about, especially not Morgan. Hadn't she hurt him enough?

"Jules, what is it?" Mom pushed.

"I missed you."

"Hey, Morgan," Mom said over Julie's shoulder.

"Mrs. Burns," he greeted with concern in his voice.

"What did you do to my daughter?" she joked.

"She fell asleep in the truck and had a bad dream."

Mom stroked Julie's back. "Probably about work. Let's get you some tea. Morgan, will you join us?"

"No," Julie said, breaking the embrace, but keeping her eyes on her mom. "He's got someplace to be."

"Nonsense. I made chocolate-chip-bacon cookies especially for you, Chief," she enticed.

"How could I say no to that?" Morgan handed Julie her backpack.

"Thanks." She grabbed it, not making eye contact. "I'm going to wash up."

"Oh, okay," Mom said.

Julie rushed up the stairs, away from the nightmare, away from Morgan.

"French vanilla or Earl Grey?" Mom called after her.

"You pick," Julie said, not looking back. She couldn't. The sight of Morgan, alive and well, standing in her hallway, would only send another wave of panic through her body.

She tossed her backpack onto the bed and padded into the bathroom. A splash of cold water would shock her out of the fright of the nightmare. Whenever she'd been awakened by a nightmare as a child, Mom would have her splash water on her cheeks. After a few seconds she and Mom would end up giggling at the mess she'd made, essentially blasting the nightmare's effects to smithereens.

She pulled her hair back into a ponytail and splashed away. Two, three, four times. Studying her reflection in the mirror she whispered, "What am I doing here?"

The nightmare made her realize she could have brought trouble to her hometown, perhaps putting innocent people in danger. Her mom. Her sister.

"Morgan," she whispered.

She'd never forgive herself if anything happened to him because of Julie's job. She'd left him years ago to give him the freedom to live his life and follow his own dreams. She knew if she'd committed to a life with him that he'd follow her to Seattle and attend college or find a job. But that wasn't his path.

His path had been to follow in his dad's footsteps and become a cop.

"Enough," she scolded herself. She had to stop thinking about the past and figure out a way to stay safe. To keep her family safe.

"Maybe I shouldn't have come home," she whispered.

But she desperately needed some time with Mom and Lana before she disappeared off the grid for good. She'd been careful to cover her tracks to prevent anyone from following her, so she'd spend a day or two here, crack her brightest smile and enjoy time spent with Mom, Lana…and Morgan.

No, being with Morgan wasn't enjoyable. It was torture.

She closed her eyes, remembering the first part of her nightmare, the feel of his hand warming hers, the kiss…

"Stop," she hushed, trying to wipe the image, the feel of their kiss out of her mind.

It did no good to remember the feeling when it wasn't real. Well, it had been real ten years ago, but she was pretty sure Morgan felt anything but love toward her right now.

Of course not. She'd broken his heart to follow her own dream. Fine, that's what she'd use as her shield. She'd talk about her fulfilling work as a counselor, but not mention how dangerous it could be. That would only worry her mom and bring out Morgan's protective instincts.

She didn't want Morgan getting involved in her life, caring too much. The nightmare drove home the consequences of that possibility.

She brushed out her long, blond hair, applied lip gloss, only because her lips were dry, and headed downstairs.

Voices drifted into the hallway as she headed for the kitchen.

"No, she hasn't mentioned anything unusually stressful at work. Why?" Mom said.

"Her nightmare made her cry out in her sleep. I'm wondering if something's troubling her."

Julie stepped into the kitchen. "Which tea did you pick?" she asked, changing the subject.

"I brewed us a white-pomegranate blend I've been wanting to try," Mom said.

"Sounds great." Julie didn't look at Morgan. Couldn't look at him for fear the image of a dead Morgan would send a shudder down her spine.

"I was asking your mother about your job," Morgan said.

"I work at Teen Life. It's great. Helping kids who really need it is so fulfilling," she said, driving home that kids around Port Whisper had no worries compared to the homeless kids she counseled in the city.

"I'll bet," he said.

She didn't expect that response. She figured he'd argue that kids in Port Whisper needed help, too. A memory of him confessing his home situation filled her with guilt. He'd opened up to her, told her that after his mom left, the revered police chief of Port Whisper had occasionally hit Morgan out of grief or frustration, and somehow Morgan felt as if it was his fault.

Julie pulled out the teacups and set them on the counter.

"What are some of your recent cases?" Morgan pressed.

Julie hesitated as she poured tea. He was fishing, trying to figure out what made her cry out in her sleep.

"Here, I'll do that," Mom said. "You sit with Morgan and catch up."

Mom kissed Julie's forehead and smiled. Mom had never given up on Morgan and Julie, especially since Morgan had never married. Julie heard he was engaged once, but it didn't work out. She wondered why.

Julie sat down across from Morgan and forced a smile. He quirked a brow. Ugh. He knew her too well.

"Well," she started, "we just had a kid placed in a really good foster home. That's always exciting."

"What about her parents?"

"His. They're drug addicts. Gave up their rights to their two sons."

"How sad," Mom said.

Julie didn't talk much about her work with her mom. She didn't want to upset her. Or scare her. Julie had found herself in threatening situations from time to time, but she was prepared.

Except for what she saw earlier this week.

Mom served the tea and slid a plate of cookies between Julie and Morgan. She joined them at the table.

"Drug addicts," Morgan said. "You deal with some pretty dangerous people."

"Says the police chief," Julie quipped.

"Police chief of a small, sleepy town."

A small, sleepy town. Her words spoken to him during one of their last fights.

"So, Morgan, how's your dad?" Mom interrupted the awkward moment.

"As well as can be expected," he said. "He's probably got only a few months."

"I'm so sorry." Julie's mom glanced into her tea.

"Yeah, well, he led a productive life," Morgan said. "Family, career, he had it all."

Insinuating Julie had given up one for another.

"Bill is a good man," Mom said.

Morgan shifted in his chair. His father appeared to be a good man to the outside world, and most of the time he was good. But Morgan and Julie knew there was another side to the chief, a dark, tortured side.

"How long are you staying around?" Morgan asked.

"A few days," Julie said. That had been the original plan, although now she wondered if everyone would be better off if she got out of town sooner rather than later.

She still didn't know how dangerous this situation was or what her pursuers wanted from her.

*Sure you do. You witnessed a crime. They want you dead.*

She shuddered.

"Honey, let me get you a sweater." Mom jumped up and went to the front hall closet.

Morgan leaned across the table, narrowing his intense, blue-green eyes at her. "Are you going to tell me what's really going on?"

She couldn't rip her gaze from his. He knew something was wrong and he wasn't going to back off. But she didn't want to involve her family or Morgan in whatever danger was stalking her, and she surely didn't need a lecture about the dangers of her job.

"It's not your problem." She got up and went to get a spoon to stir sugar into her tea.

"It is my problem if you're in trouble and you've brought it to my town."

She closed her eyes. Right. It was about Morgan protecting his citizens, not about him being worried about her.

Julie was about to tell him to mind his own business when Mom breezed into the kitchen.

"Here you go," her mom said, hesitating. She glanced from Morgan to Julie. "What's going on?"

"Nothing, Mom. Everything's fine," Julie said.

With a shake of his head, Morgan downed his tea and stood. "Thanks for the tea and cookies, Mrs. Burns."

"You're very welcome," Mom said with a questioning frown.

"Good night." With a nod Morgan left, shutting the front door with a resounding click.

Julie sighed and closed her eyes.

"Jules, sweetie, talk to me." Mom placed her hand on Julie's shoulder.

"I'm just burned out at work."

"Julie?"

She glanced at her mom.

"I love you with all my heart," Mom said. "I think a part of Morgan's heart still loves you, too. We're worried—"

"I'm fine," Julie snapped, sitting at the kitchen table.

Mom walked up to her and rubbed her shoulders. "Whatever it is, we can work it out together."

Julie wasn't so sure. If the police couldn't help Julie, Mom and Morgan surely couldn't. Nor did she want to get them involved with whatever criminal element was stalking her.

She loved her mom too much.

Which would make it that much harder to leave again. But she had to. She couldn't risk trouble following her here, to her mom's house, to Morgan's town.

"Honey, please," her mother pleaded.

"Something happened at work."

"Do you want to talk about it?"

Julie shook her head. "I can't. Not yet."

Mom frowned. "Well, you'll tell me when you're ready. But, sweetie, you can't run from your problems. You should know that."

Was she referring to Suzy's death? Or to Morgan?

Sadness washed over her. So much loss.

Mom stroked Julie's hair. "It's okay. You're home now. And Lana can't wait to see you."

"I can't wait to see her, either."

"She's coming for breakfast."

"Awesome." And it was. Julie kept so busy at work that she had little time to miss them. But right now, sitting in Mom's floral kitchen, she remembered the joy and laughter they'd shared. An ache crawled through her chest.

"You look exhausted. How about I tuck you in?" Mom offered.

"That would be great."

Morgan pulled out of the Burnses' driveway, but didn't go far. Parking a few houses down from the old Victorian, he eyed the upstairs window. Julie's room.

He guessed whatever made her scream out in her sleep was the same thing that drove her back home to the safety of family and friends. And now she was having second thoughts.

He could read it in her eyes.

It still amazed him how connected they were after all these years. Why didn't she trust him enough to ask for his help? Because he still wasn't good enough? He was only a small-town cop and she needed...what?

He whipped out his cell phone and called Ethan Beck, an old friend who was a detective with the Seattle Police Department.

"Beck."

"Hey, E, it's Morgan Wright."

"As in Chief Morgan Wright?"

"Knock it off."

Morgan and Ethan had recently reconnected thanks to another old friend, Jake Walters.

"Good to hear from you, man," Ethan said. "Jake told me you were chief pooh-bah out there in Port Whisper. How's that goin'?"

"It has its good days and bad." Like today. "Listen, I need a favor."

"Name it."

"An old friend's returned to town and I think she's in trouble."

"Is she cute? Available?"

"Yes and no."

"Really?" Ethan teased.

"Can you check your database for anything on Julie Burns, female, twenty-eight? Seattle social worker for Teen Life."

"You mean *the* Julie Burns?"

"Yup."

"What am I looking for?"

"I'm not sure."

"You think she's into something criminal?"

The terror in her golden eyes flashed across his mind. "No, but my gut tells me she's in trouble."

"I'll see what I can find."

"Thanks."

"Sure. You hear about Jake and Robin? They're engaged."

Morgan took a deep breath. "No, I hadn't heard. That's great news."

"How soon do you need this information about Julie?"

"As soon as you can get it."

"Check. Take care, buddy."

"You, too."

Morgan ended the call and dropped the phone on the seat beside him. Staring up at Julie's room, he leaned back and considered what could be going on with his fragile ex-girlfriend.

She was suffering from some kind of post-trauma issue, that's for sure. Maybe her work had finally gotten to her, listening to the gut-wrenching stories of abused teenagers, counseling them, hoping they'd find a better life, only to have them return to an abusive living situation.

It had to get to her, haunt her dreams, trigger nightmares.

Yet she'd called out Morgan's name when she'd awakened from the nightmare in his truck.

Maybe she'd been dreaming about one of their last fights, the harsh words he'd uttered out of sheer agony of losing the one person he'd trusted most.

He wondered what life would have looked like had he followed her to Seattle, left his father and chosen another line of work. But his life was here, making his father proud, earning his respect and protecting the citizens of Port Whisper.

It had been his destiny.

At one point he thought Julie had been a part of that destiny.

"Get over it already." He thought he had. He'd fallen in love with Renee, at least he thought it was love, and he'd appreciated Anna's company, her bright smile and sense of humor.

Seeing Jules again, rescuing her from whatever threat was stalking her, brought it all back to the surface.

Regret burned in his chest. No, he'd done the right thing by letting her go to follow her dream. The pit in his stomach said otherwise.

He clicked the radio on and tapped his fingers against the steering wheel. Something told him to stay close. He had tomorrow off. He could go the night without sleep.

Even if he went home and climbed into bed, he knew he wouldn't sleep, not with the image of Julie's frightened eyes haunting him.

"You're going to tell me what's going on," he whispered, eyeing her bedroom.

The light went off. He took a deep breath and considered his next move. He'd see what Ethan turned up and he'd go from there.

Tomorrow he'd confront Julie about her situation, but under no uncertain terms would he discuss their past. This was business. He was the police chief sworn to protect the people of Port Whisper.

As long as Jules was here, she was under his protection just like everyone else.

A vibrating sound awakened her from a deep sleep. She opened her eyes and spotted her cell phone dancing across the nightstand. The bedside clock read four-thirty. She flipped on the lamp and grabbed her phone, recognizing the caller ID as William's work number. William and Julie had consulted with one another on unusually complicated cases. But why call at such an odd time?

"William?" she answered.

Silence.

"William?"

"You can run, Blondie," a gravelly voice said. "But we're always right behind you."

She jackknifed in bed. "Who is this?"

The line went dead and a surge of panic ripped through her. Fearing for William's safety, she called his cell. She paced her room as it rang. Two, three times.

"Hello?" he answered groggily.

She sighed and shifted onto the bed.

"You're okay," she said.

"Julie? It's—" he hesitated "—four in the morning."

"I know, I'm sorry."

"Why wouldn't I be okay?"

"I just got a threatening phone call from your work number."

"A threatening call? I don't understand."

"I'm in trouble, William. Ever since I witnessed Dane's kidnapping, strange things have been happening: hang-ups, the office break-in, and I think someone's been following me."

"Call the police."

"What can they do? Put a twenty-four-hour

watch on my apartment? No, I have to disappear for a while."

"Where are you going?"

"I don't know yet. I'll be in touch."

"Julie—"

She ended the call, and nervously paced to the window.

*We're always right behind you.*

Which meant they were trailing her to Port Whisper? How? She'd taken her personal files with her mom's contact information from the office. Morgan said no one had followed them from the ferry. She glanced at her phone. Were they tracking her through a GPS chip? Had they already found her?

She had no choice. She had to run. And destroy her phone along the way.

Julie packed up her things. There was a commuter bus that stopped in town around six. She'd catch it and head west to a larger town, like Port Angeles, where she could blend in.

She flipped off her bedroom light and padded across the hall to Mom's room. As she peered inside, she realized if she woke Mom she'd only talk her out of leaving. But Julie had made up her mind. She didn't want to risk bringing trouble to Port Whisper and put the townspeople in danger.

She tiptoed downstairs, glancing across the

warm and welcoming living room. Sadness welled up in her chest as she remembered the many Christmases she'd enjoyed in this very room. She'd had a wonderful childhood, safe and happy, unlike the kids she counseled. Julie thought she'd been doing the honorable thing when she'd left for the city. She had the solid upbringing and faith in God that grounded her and gave her strength to help the kids at Teen Life. Faith that had been tested, ripped apart and destroyed as she watched one kid after another fail.

It was on those days that Julie missed the comfort and innocence of Port Whisper.

Innocence that would be destroyed if her stalker tracked her here. Andy Trotter was missing. She'd seen Dane Simms being shoved into a van. She didn't know what was going on, but she knew witnessing the abduction had put her life at risk.

She placed a note on the hall table, opened the front door and slipped outside. The cool morning chill slapped her cheeks as she started down the porch steps. She'd catch the commuter bus and head to Port Angeles, find a safe place to hide and…

What? Get a job in a burger joint? Take a nanny job? She hadn't thought past getting away and escaping the threat.

As she headed down Oak Street she thought about her childhood friends from the youth club, Carrie, Megan and Taylor.

And Suzy.

There wasn't a day that passed when she didn't think about Suzy.

"Don't go there," she muttered, flipping her collar up against the breeze. The hair on the back of her neck bristled.

She narrowed her eyes and focused ahead, looking for signs of danger.

*Don't be paranoid. It's Port Whisper.*

*A small, sleepy little town,* Morgan had said yesterday in the kitchen, repeating her words from their fight years ago.

She'd intentionally kept Morgan at a distance, yet somehow he was still able to sense her fear. Another reason to leave town. If she saw him again, he'd do his best to break down the wall she'd lodged between them.

The brisk walk to town brightened her spirits a bit, if that was possible. Watching the sunrise had always been a treat, especially when she'd shared it with Morgan, his arm around her, humming in her ear.

She could never watch a sunrise without thinking of him, or remembering the time they were questioned by a cop at Squamish Harbor. They'd fallen asleep while waiting for the sunrise.

Turning the corner to the town center, she eyed a spot behind the post office where she could wait until the bus came. The post office overlooked the water, so peaceful at this time of the morning.

She shook herself out of the false sense of peace. She had to plan her next move. Her phantom caller threatened to be right behind her. Even if he didn't find Julie, chances were whoever was after her would keep abducting kids, kids who didn't seem to matter to anyone but her.

The kids sometimes reminded her of Morgan before they'd started dating. He'd had his share of challenges—a learning disability, an absent mother—which had led to anger issues and fights in school. Somehow Julie had gotten through to him and they'd fallen in love.

After she left she'd worried that he'd slip into that dark place again. But the night he'd told her they would marry someday, he'd also said that he'd changed. Because of her.

That was the first time she felt she'd had a positive impact on someone's life. She surely didn't have one on Suzy's.

She tossed her phone into the water, figuring that would destroy the GPS. All her contacts, photos and text messages…gone. But she had to get used to being alone. She eyed Sahalish

Island across the water, uninhabited except for tourists who visited for the day or campers who sailed onto the small shore and pitched tents in the rugged terrain. The island reminded her of her baby sister, Lana, who ran Delightful Tours, a business that took visitors to the island, out of a snack shop called Stone Soup. Lana was never going to forgive Julie for leaving town without seeing her.

*This is so messed up.*

She wished she could pray to God to tell her she was doing the right thing, but she'd given up on prayer somewhere around the fourth year in her job. Where was God when horrible things were happening to these kids?

Out of the corner of her eye she spotted a tall, male figure step around the corner. Glancing away, she shoved her hands into her jacket pockets and wandered in the other direction. Calm, casual.

She climbed down the rocks to the shore, remembering a path she and Morgan used to take when strolling along the water to the main dock. They would hide out beneath the pier, steal a kiss, confess their fears and share their dreams for the future.

"Miss?" the man called after her.

She picked up her pace. She'd given directions to the guy at the ferry and he'd found her on the boat. But Morgan said no one had followed them from the ferry, right?

"Hey, wait!" the man called.

She broke into a full-blown sprint. Not easy considering the unstable rocks beneath her feet. She never should have come back here, should have known better. She shot a glance over her shoulder at the guy, who stood on the pier, watching, but not following her.

She turned and slammed into something hard and firm.

The man's partner?

"Where do you think you're going?"

# Chapter Three

"Let go of me!" She struggled against Morgan's grip, as if fearing for her life.

"Julie, stop!" Morgan ordered. "It's me, Morgan."

She hesitated, still clutching his jacket, and glanced up. "Morgan? What are you doing here?"

"Apparently, stopping you from running away." He hesitated. "Again."

He couldn't believe it. She didn't have the decency to stay a few days and catch up with her family. She didn't have the decency to say goodbye.

Some things never changed.

"What are you doing down here?" he said, but he had a pretty good idea.

"I'm… I couldn't sleep so I went for a walk."

"Uh-huh. With your backpack?" He released

her, but she clung to his jacket for a second longer than necessary.

Then she let go. "Are you stalking me?"

"That's an odd way of putting it."

"How did you know I was here?" She took a step back, then shot a nervous glance over her shoulder.

"I saw you leave the house."

"You were watching me?"

"Hey, Chief! She okay?" the man called from the pier.

Morgan waved. "She's fine, Ray, thanks."

"Who's that?" Julie asked.

"Don't you remember Ray Carlisle? He owns Klinger Drugs?"

"I... I didn't recognize him."

More like she assumed he was out to hurt her.

"We need to talk." Morgan glanced at his watch. "The Turnstyle staff is usually there by now. Let's get some coffee."

"No, I have to..."

"What? Catch a bus?"

She glanced at the water. With his forefinger and thumb to her chin, he turned her face to look him in the eye. "You were going where, exactly? And you were skipping out on your mom?"

Her golden eyes challenged him. "It's none of your business."

"You're in my town. It's my business. Now, come on." He motioned for her to take the next set of stairs up to the street level.

Ethan had called Morgan with some interesting information. Jules had reported a missing teenager, a week later reported an abduction of a second boy and her office had been broken into.

Morgan guessed whatever was going on had motivated her return to Port Whisper, and her escape number this morning.

Escape. That's how she'd described leaving town ten years ago. She'd wanted to escape small-town life and do something important.

Whatever important work she was into had landed her in trouble. Ethan said the cops were looking into the abduction but it wasn't easy tracking kids who didn't want to be found. They also had no leads on the office break-in.

It wouldn't be easy confronting Julie about her situation. He assumed she hadn't shared the details with her mother. Jules tended to be like that, wanting to help others, but not being able to accept help in return.

They walked in silence the two blocks to the Turnstyle Coffee Shop. The sign read Closed, but he knew Anna and Lew, the owner, were prepping to open. They always opened for him if he needed a cup of caffeine. Today he needed more than just one. He wanted to be clearheaded so he could interrogate Julie and get answers.

"They're not open yet," she said, shoving her hands into her jacket pockets.

Morgan tapped on the window. Anna poked her head out of the kitchen, waved and headed for the door. She was a nice woman and Morgan enjoyed spending time with her, yet he'd been up front with Anna, told her he wasn't ready for a serious relationship. He sensed she ignored his warning.

Anna swung open the door, her eyes brightening. "Hi, Morgan." They hugged and he broke it off a little quicker than usual.

"Anna, this is Julie Burns. Julie, Anna."

As the women shook hands, Anna narrowed her eyes. "Burns as in Edith's daughter?"

"Yes," Julie said.

Anna shot Morgan a quick glance. She knew, as did most everyone in town, about Morgan and Julie. Once upon a time they were in love, named the couple most likely to marry, settle down and raise a family in Port Whisper.

"Nice to meet you," Anna said.

"Coffee ready?" Morgan asked.

"You bet. Come in."

Morgan motioned for Julie to slide into a booth.

"You want coffee too, Julie?"

"Sure."

With an odd curl of her lips, Anna headed back to the kitchen.

"You dated her, didn't you?" Julie said.

"I'm the one asking the questions."

"Morgan—"

"I spoke with the Seattle P.D."

Julie leaned back in the booth and crossed her arms over her chest. "Why?"

"Because I need to know what's going on if I'm going to protect you."

"I don't need your protection." She glanced out the window.

"No? Then what do you need?"

"To catch the commuter bus and get out of town."

"What will that accomplish?"

She shrugged.

"No more shrugging, silent treatment and crossing your arms over your chest. It's time to be honest with me, Jules. I know you filed a police report about a missing boy, I know about the break-in at work and I know you reported an abduction. Fill me in here."

She looked straight at him. "No."

"No?"

"I can't divulge that kind of information."

"I'm not asking for personal information

about the teenagers. I'm asking about what you reported to police. And why you ran."

"Here you go," Anna said, sliding two coffee mugs on the table. She poured Morgan's coffee, then Julie's. "So, you in town long?"

"No," Jules answered.

"Yes," Morgan countered.

"Okay, then." Anna eyed them. "Just yell if you need a warm-up."

Julie's gaze followed Anna into the back, as if making sure she was out of earshot.

"Spill it," Morgan said.

"I don't want to get you involved in this. I probably shouldn't have come back. I realize that now."

"But you did. Why?"

"I don't know, I guess… I was scared. I felt threatened so I came home where it's—"

"Boring?" he interrupted.

"Safe."

Morgan sipped his coffee. Studied her. It surprised him that she still felt a connection to Port Whisper. He figured she'd put this quaint little town behind her when she'd moved to the city.

"Judging from your behavior, I'm assuming someone's after you?" Morgan asked.

"I think so. After I reported the abduction I noticed someone following me on the way home from work. I've also been getting threatening calls. I got one this morning."

"Where's your cell? Maybe we can trace the call."

"I threw it in the Sound in case they could trace the GPS signal."

"Smart girl." Thinking defensively would go a long way to keeping her safe.

"Then there was the break-in at work," she said.

"What did they take when they broke into your office?"

"Files, mostly."

"Your files?"

"Some, but I keep others at home, as well."

"Continue."

"I felt like I was being followed yesterday, so after a dinner meeting I hopped the ferry. Then I got a text—*I see you.* A guy I'd given directions to on the street was looking at his phone, then he looked at me and smiled." She closed her eyes and shuddered.

Morgan wanted to slide into the booth next to her and put his arm around her. He took another swig of coffee.

"You were running away from him on the ferry. That's when you tripped and fell?" Morgan said.

"Yes." She glanced at him. "And you were

there." A content smile played at the corner of her lips.

He ignored it. "Do you think he's a part of this?"

"I don't know."

Neither did Morgan, but as a precaution he'd kept a close watch on his rearview mirror last night to make sure no one had followed them from the ferry. "Supposing someone is after you, what do they want?" Morgan asked.

"I don't know."

"Jules," he said, in a warning tone.

"I really don't, Morgan. I don't even know who these people are. I can only guess it's related to the boys."

"Tell me a little about them."

"I can't. It's a confidentiality thing."

"Tough. You need to confide in me so I can save your life."

There, he said it. He knew the endgame in these types of situations was often murder. One of her clients was missing, perhaps dead, and another had been kidnapped right in front of her. What did she think was going to happen if the mysterious "they" found her?

"I really need to catch that bus," she said.

"For where?"

"Port Angeles."

"What happens when you get to Port Angeles?"

"I'll get a job, I guess."

"What about your counseling job?"

"I left town without telling anyone, so I'm sure I'll be out of a job by the time I get back. If I ever get back."

"You can't run from your problems, Jules. They always find you."

She stirred cream into her coffee, circling the edges of the cup with her spoon. Morgan opened three packets of sugar and poured them into her mug.

She cracked a smile. "You remembered."

"I remember a lot of things." Like her hurtful words when she'd tried to break it off with him. He'd thought he'd talked her out of it. He hadn't.

"What do you remember about the night you witnessed the abduction?" he asked.

"I really don't want to—"

"Look, you'll never outrun these guys and they won't stop until they get what they want. We need to figure out what that is."

"I think they want me dead."

Sure, he'd thought the same thing, but hearing her say it made it more real. He leaned back in the booth, fighting the panic knotting his gut. "Why do you say that?"

"I filed the missing-persons report for Andy. I witnessed Dane being abducted."

"But the police hit a dead end. They've closed that file. No, there's something more going on here. What is it?"

"I don't know, okay!" She closed her eyes.

Anna poked her head around the corner. "Need a refill on those coffees?"

"We're good, thanks," Morgan said.

"I'm sorry," Julie whispered.

A part of him wished she were apologizing for abandoning him instead of the outburst.

"Look, if I'm going to keep you safe, you need to be completely honest," he said.

She glanced at him with fear in her eyes. Why? What else was she hiding?

"Do you have any files with you now?" he asked.

"Yes, in my backpack."

"Good, we'll start there."

"Start what?"

"Trying to piece this together."

"I don't want to involve you in this."

"Why, because you care about me?" He wanted to snap the words back the minute they left his lips. He wasn't cruel by nature, but he was frustrated that he might not be able to protect her because she was fighting him every step of the way.

Silence stretched between them. He clenched his jaw and stared out the diner window.

"Morgan?" she said.

He glanced at her.

"I *am* sorry," she said.

He knew she wasn't referring to the current threat. Tough. He couldn't deal with that right now. "Let's focus on the present situation. Forget the past. Ready to go?" He slid out of the booth and waited.

"Sure."

He dropped a ten-dollar bill on the table and started for the door. As he opened it for her, she hesitated and looked at him with those enchanting golden eyes. "If you figure out how to forget the past let me know, because I never have."

She strolled past him onto the sidewalk.

As he watched her step to the curb and glance across town, he realized he needed to solve this case fast so he could put her on a ferry and send her to Seattle before he lost touch with reality and started dreaming again.

Dreaming of a charmed life with his high-school sweetheart.

Julie had wondered if leaving him would cause Morgan's bad-boy tendencies to surface. When Mom told her Morgan had joined the service, earned his college degree and returned to become police chief, Julie figured he'd moved on and conquered the darkness.

Sitting across from his desk, she realized something else had changed: Morgan had become a master at closing himself off. It was as if he flipped a switch from charismatic chief to hardened detective. He was hyper-focused on solving the case the Seattle P.D. had been unable to get traction on. Not because Morgan was worried about Julie, but, she guessed, because he wanted to solve it so he could keep his citizens safe, and get Julie out of his life.

He hated her that much.

"Andy Trotter was a dealer? Of what?" he asked, leafing through a file.

She felt guilty showing him the boys' personal files but she knew he was right: the more information he had, the better chance he had of piecing together some answers.

He glanced up, waiting for a response. His eyes grew dark blue and intense. Cold.

"Crack cocaine, mostly. Some heroin," she said.

"Which means he worked for some pretty bad people. But the kid was homeless? Didn't dealing give him enough money to live?"

"The kids get addicted themselves and end up spending their money on their habit."

He fingered a sheet of paper. "I realize dealing drugs can be deadly, but why abduct a kid?"

"I didn't see Andy being abducted. He just disappeared."

"Tell me about Dane's abduction." He leaned back in his chair and tapped a pencil on his desk.

He was in cop mode, questioning her like any other witness.

"I was going to one of the flophouses Dane frequented. When I turned the corner, I spotted two men shoving him into the back of a van. I called out—"

"You what?" He leaned forward.

"Instinct, okay?"

"Did they see you?"

"I'm not sure. Anyway, I dialed 9-1-1 and watched the van tear off. I'll never forget the sound of Dane's voice screaming to let him go."

"Did it sound like he knew them? Did he call them by name?"

"I'm not sure."

"Think, Jules. Close your eyes and replay the scene in your head."

With a sigh, she did as he asked. It had been a cool, blustery day in Seattle, and when she'd turned the corner she was fastening the top button on her coat.

Dane cried out, snapping her attention to the

alley. She froze at the sight of two men practically ripping off Dane's jacket to subdue him as he kicked and screamed.

*Damn it, let me go! I didn't do it, Henson. I didn't do it!*

Julie snapped her eyes open. "Henson, he called one of the guys Henson."

"Good. It's a start." He picked up the phone.

"Who are you calling?"

"Detective Beck. You remember Ethan? He's a Seattle cop."

"Oh, right."

She wished she would have known that before. She always liked Ethan, one of the Three Musketeers, as they'd called themselves growing up. Ethan and his friend Jake would vacation in Port Whisper every summer, and Morgan always looked forward to seeing them. As teenagers Morgan and Julie saw less of the guys from the other side of the water. She was glad Morgan had kept in touch with Ethan.

"I've got a name," Morgan said into the phone. "Henson. Yeah…no…" He glanced at Julie. "I doubt it. Sure, thanks." He hung up and eyed Julie. "He's going to look into it. In the meantime we need to figure out a way to keep you safe."

"What about my mom?"

"Need to keep her safe, too."

"She'll want to lock me up and not let me go back to Seattle."

"Is that so bad?"

"Look, I know you love it here, but—"

"All I'm saying is, a few weeks off or even a month away from your work could be a good thing. I can see it's sucking the energy out of you."

"I was fine until Andy disappeared and Dane was abducted."

Morgan quirked a brow.

"What?" she said.

"How long have you been at this?"

"Six years."

"When was the last time you took a vacation?"

"Last spring."

"Really? Where'd you go?"

She hesitated and he smirked.

"Omaha," she snapped.

"For a vacation?"

"Okay, fine. I went for a conference."

"I rest my case."

"I wish you'd get off my case." Probably because he was right. Her job was sucking the life from her and she didn't know what to do about it.

"Let's talk about your safety," Morgan said. "We should get you out of your mom's house."

"What? No."

"It's temporary. You can stay at Dad's place. I've been working on it."

"No, I couldn't—"

"Sure you could." He scribbled something on a piece of paper.

"Mom won't agree."

"She will when we explain the situation."

Julie sighed. "I hate involving her in this."

"Too late, you already have."

Anger rose in her chest. "Stop doing that."

"What?"

"Making me feel guilty for coming back and bringing my work baggage with me. I thought I'd covered my tracks."

"That's not what I'm trying to do."

"No? You want me to feel bad about coming back, you're punishing me for—"

"I'm stating the truth—you landed in trouble. You got scared and came back to the one place where you feel safe. That's okay, Jules, but you have to forgive yourself for coming home."

She was speechless, didn't know how to respond to that one. "You're right, I guess."

Their eyes locked and she couldn't bring herself to break the connection. He wasn't trying to make her feel worse than she already did. He was trying to stop her from beating herself up.

As only Morgan could do.

His desk phone rang and he grabbed it, breaking the connection between them. She took a deep breath, realizing she'd been holding it.

"Chief Wright," he said in a deep, clipped voice. "That was fast. What?" Morgan leaned back in his chair and ran his hand slowly down his face.

She knew that expression, one of utter frustration.

"Thanks for letting me know." He dropped the receiver onto the cradle.

"What?" she pushed.

"The boy you reported missing, Andy Trotter?"

"Yeah."

"They think they found his body in an alley."

# Chapter Four

Julie sucked in a quick breath and gripped the edge of Morgan's desk. She couldn't quite process what he'd just said. Andy was dead?

"Jules, breathe." Morgan came around to her side of the desk and placed his hand on her shoulder. "Look at me."

She glanced up through teary eyes.

"It's not your fault," he said.

He knew her too well, knew she was going to that place where she felt responsible, felt as if somehow she could have saved the teenager.

As if she should have saved Suzy.

"I knew he was struggling," she said. "But I didn't think he'd end up...dead."

"Come on, we need to get you home and talk to your mom." They started for the door. "Ethan asked if you could ID the body."

She absently nodded and must have looked

upset, because Morgan squeezed her hand. She glanced into his eyes.

"I'll be right beside you," he said.

"Thanks. I just... Thanks, I guess."

They went outside and got into his truck. Her heart swelled with grief as she gradually accepted Andy's death. It was her job to save these kids, stop them from being sucked into the vortex of the drug world. Sure, she'd acknowledged the fact she wouldn't be able to save all of them, but Andy was special. She fingered the butterfly locket around her neck, a gift from Andy for her birthday. Even though it had been on the wrong day, the wrong month, he said he wanted to make sure he didn't miss it, and presented her with the silver locket. He'd even shown her a receipt to prove he didn't steal it, that he'd legitimately bought it at a flea market.

Julie didn't make a habit of accepting gifts from her clients, but made an exception in Andy's case. He really wanted to get clean and live a healthy life, find a job and have a family. It seemed important to him that she accept his gift. She swallowed back the ball rising in her throat.

"Jules?"

"Hmm?" she answered, gazing out the window.

"That's a nice locket. Who gave it to you? A boyfriend?"

"I don't have time to date. Andy gave it to me."

"It really isn't your fault. You have to believe that."

She glanced at Morgan. He offered a sympathetic smile.

"I know that, intellectually, but emotionally…" She shook her head and glanced back out the window. It was bad enough that she'd been unable to save Andy, but worse, Morgan witnessed her failure, making it that much more painful.

She'd abandoned Morgan to save teenagers and for what? Andy's body was on a slab somewhere, his dreams and hopes dead with him.

Morgan reached over and placed his hand on top of hers. The compassionate gesture irritated her. She didn't want his compassion; she didn't deserve it.

"You give these kids hope, Jules, a way out, but it's up to them to follow the light."

She wanted the resentful Morgan back, the one who'd remind her what a failure she was. A flurry of anger welled in her chest. She wanted to hit something or scream.

"He's at peace, with our Lord in heaven," Morgan consoled.

"You sure about that?" she challenged, ripping her hand from his. "I mean, if God didn't see fit to care about him in life, what makes you think He'll welcome him into heaven, huh?"

Morgan didn't answer, probably a good thing, since anything he said would only infuriate her more.

"Looks like your mom's got company," he said, pulling up the driveway.

Julie glanced out the front window and recognized her sister's VW Bug. Not good. Julie didn't want to go into the house like this, an emotional wreck. She'd always been the good-natured child, grounded and ambitious, while Lana struggled with moodiness and disorganization. If Mom and Lana saw her like this, her emotions a tangled mess, it would freak them out.

She shot a glance at Morgan, who pulled up and parked in front of the house. Why wasn't he freaked by her outburst?

"Lana will be happy to see you," Morgan said.

Julie got out of the car, but headed in the opposite direction of the house.

"Jules," he said, following her. "I thought we agreed, you aren't running away."

"I need a minute—can I just have a minute alone to get my head together before I go in there?" She kept marching, but he didn't fall back. She stopped and planted her hands on her hips. "Alone means alone."

"Not happening, not until this thing is resolved."

"This isn't high school, Morgan. I'm not your responsibility." She almost choked on the words as they left her lips. The pained expression on his face made her turn her back to him. "I'm sorry. I don't know why I said that."

He touched her shoulder again, only this time the contact dissolved her angst slightly. Every time he touched her she simultaneously felt joy and pain, the two warring for victory.

"You're upset about Andy," he said.

She jerked around to face him. "Which doesn't justify lashing out at you in such a mean-spirited way."

"No, it doesn't." They stood there for a good minute, her shame pooling between them.

"I don't want Mom and Lana to see me like this," she finally said.

"They're your family. They'll love you no matter what."

*I'll love you no matter what, Jules.*

She wondered if he remembered he'd said those same words to her just days before she'd left.

"We should go in." He offered his hand and

she took it, appreciating the warm, solid connection.

They walked up the driveway to the house and she relaxed her fingers, giving him permission to let go. He didn't. He held on to her as if to say he wasn't going anywhere. No matter what she'd done to him in the past, he'd be there for her.

She didn't deserve his forgiveness.

"Awesome! Mom, they're holding hands!" Lana called over her shoulder from the porch, then raced down the steps and wrapped her arms around Julie's neck. "I've missed you, big sister." Lana rocked side to side, and Morgan let Julie go.

Lana stepped back and clapped her hands. "My prayers came true. I'm so excited."

"What prayers?" Mom asked.

"Please, let's all go inside," Morgan coached, glancing across the property. "We need to discuss a few things."

"Like a wedding date?" Lana looped her arm through Julie's and led her up the stairs. "The best Christmas present ever. Please make it a spring wedding. And outside, like at the Port Whisper Inn. Caroline's gardens are beautiful."

Overwhelmed with Lana's enthusiasm, Julie could hardly get a word in edgewise.

"A wedding?" Mom said leading them into

the kitchen. "That was quick. She hasn't even been home for twenty-four hours."

"There's no wedding," Julie corrected. "Lana jumped to conclusions."

"But you were holding hands."

They found spots around the kitchen table, Lana barely able to control her burst of energy. She was still hopeful that Morgan and Julie would get back together.

"Were you two off watching the sunrise?" Mom asked. "Remember how they used to set their alarms for five and head down to Squamish Harbor Point to watch the sun rise?" she said to Lana.

"So romantic." Lana grinned at Julie.

"We weren't watching the sunrise."

"But you were gone so early," her mom said.

"I was leaving town."

"What?" Mom gasped.

"Without seeing me?" Lana added.

Julie glanced at Morgan and he nodded his encouragement.

"I think something that happened at work has put me in danger. I came back home to distance myself from things, and apparently I've only made it worse."

"What do you mean, worse?" Mom asked.

"I think they might be tracking me to Port Whisper."

"Who are they?" Lana questioned.

"I'm not even sure."

"One of the boys you counsel?" Mom asked.

"No, but a few of the boys are involved. I'd rather not get into too much detail."

"We got word just now that one of the teenagers she works with was found dead this morning," Morgan said.

"Oh, Julie, I'm so sorry." Mom reached over and stroked Julie's shoulder.

"I took all personal information from my office to prevent anyone from finding me here, but I got a threatening call this morning on my cell, which made me think they could track the GPS chip in my phone."

"So she took off, not wanting to put the two of you in danger," Morgan offered. He was backing her up. Why?

"And you brought her back," Mom said.

"Running away never solved anything," Morgan said. "You keep running and they keep chasing."

"What should she do, Chief?" Mom asked.

"Just to be safe, we should move you out of this house."

"But Mom's not in danger," Lana protested.

"We can't risk it," Morgan said. "There's plenty of room at Dad's place and I'd feel better if you both were close so I can keep an eye on you."

"I don't know, Morgan. I watch the Kotter twins after school three days a week, and I don't think Angela could find alternate child care on short notice," Mom said.

"You can watch them at Dad's house." Morgan turned to Lana. "And I'd prefer if you don't go anywhere alone, Lana. Keep an eye out for strangers hanging around your shop."

"Oh, okay, sure."

"You should move in with your mom and Julie, too," Morgan pressed.

"No way. I'm fine above the shop. There are always people around town."

As Julie watched the plan unfold, her chest ached with regret. "I'm sorry, I'm so sorry."

Mom stroked Julie's back.

"No, no, no." Lana came around the table and hugged Julie from behind. "Don't go there. We're just glad to have you home, even if you brought drama with you."

Julie glanced at Lara and a sparkle lit Lara's gray-green eyes. "The three of us can do anything together, especially with the chief's help, right?"

Julie hesitated and Lana poked her in the ribs, Julie's tickle spot.

"Don't." Julie smiled and jerked away.

"Right?" Lana prompted.

"Right."

The three of them had conquered just about everything after Julie and Lana's father had died when they were teenagers. Her mom thought that's what set off Lana's moodiness, yet Julie had gritted her teeth and kept it together, put her head down and kept her grades up, her aspirations high. Dad would have wanted it that way, and Mom didn't need two kids who were a wreck. It was bad enough that Mom had lost her husband.

"Morgan, are you sure it's okay with your dad if we take over his house?" Mom asked.

"He'd be honored if you'd use it as your safe house, and quite frankly, I'm good with the construction aspect of things, but could use a woman's touch to liven up the place. It's kind of... dark."

Dark, like his dad's moods when no one was around. Jules heard the inference.

"The truth comes out," Lana joked. "He's going to put you two to work."

"I didn't mean—"

"Just kidding, Chief," Lana said.

"How long will we be staying?" Mom asked.

"No way to know for sure. Plan on a week."

"Well, if we're out of the house, I could

have Trevor take a run at my hardwood floors. They're in bad shape," Mom said.

"Always seeing the bright side." Julie smiled up at her mom.

"We should get you set up as soon as possible," Morgan said. "Julie got the call a few hours ago, and although we don't know if they can track the GPS chip in her phone, they could be on their way. Pack in terms of a week. I can always come back if you need something."

"I'll help." Lana stood. She and Mom headed for the second floor.

"I'll be there in a sec," Julie said.

They disappeared up the stairs.

"Morgan, listen, I know this is incredibly uncomfortable—"

"It's fine," he said, pulling out his cell phone. "I've gotta make a few calls. Can I tell Ethan we'll be there around two?"

He kept his eyes trained on the phone.

"Sure, that's fine," Julie said, frustrated that he'd shut her down. She wanted to thank him, apologize again...give him a hug.

Uh-oh.

He glanced at her. "You'd better help them pack. I need to run a few errands. I'll be back in a bit."

"Okay." Breaking eye contact, she headed for the stairs, frustrated yet relieved that he didn't let her wander down an emotional road that could only lead to disaster, to Julie falling into his arms.

That could never be. There was too much pain associated with their relationship, and he'd never understood her need to do something bigger for humanity, like counsel runaways.

Even after this crisis was resolved, there was no way to go back, to repair their damaged relationship, a relationship meant to stay in the past.

She had to focus on her future and staying alive.

It wasn't until they walked through Dad's front door that Morgan realized Julie hadn't seen the inside of his house. Never knowing what mood his dad would be in on any given day, Morgan couldn't risk it.

As Julie scanned the dark living room, filled with dark furniture, a cherrywood bookcase spanning the wall and black leather furniture, he realized to an outsider it must look awfully, well, depressing. Her gaze landed on Dad's recliner, positioned directly across from the television. Dad was in his own world when he sat there, eating pretzels out of a plastic bowl, watching the news. A scene replayed itself in Morgan's mind: the day Morgan and Dad got into a fight over Morgan's C in history. His father had lectured that Morgan needed the grades to get into college, but at that point Morgan didn't care.

He hadn't met Julie yet.

"If you painted the walls a lighter shade it would really brighten things up," Edith offered, jerking him out of his flashback.

"Yeah, sorry. I know it's pretty depressing in here," Morgan offered.

"It's not depressing, just, well, male," Edith joked. "You sure your father won't mind us changing things?"

It had been fifteen years since a woman worked her magic in the house. It was long overdue.

"He won't mind," Morgan said. "I'll probably sell it when…" His voice trailed off. "Well, eventually I'll have to sell. I've got a place of my own down the block."

Dad was dying. Morgan didn't talk about it much, and tried not thinking about the hole it would leave in his life. Morgan had grown up with one goal in mind after his mother left: make his dad proud.

Julie placed her hand on Morgan's arm as if she read his thoughts. He clenched his jaw to steel himself from her touch. He resented it, feeling vulnerable all over again. She would leave him again, after this case was resolved. He couldn't let her get too close.

Breaking contact, he headed for the stairs. "Rooms are up here."

He led them to the three bedrooms upstairs, which suddenly looked bleak when he saw them through the women's eyes. "Here's Dad's room. Edith, you can stay in here. I'll change the sheets before Julie and I head into Seattle."

"Just leave them out," Edith said. "I can do that."

"And across the hall is my room," he continued.

Jules stepped up beside him, but he didn't look at her. Dad hadn't changed Morgan's room much since he'd left for the service, then college. After graduation, Morgan spent a few years with the King County Sheriff's Department, then Dad got sick, and Morgan decided to apply for his job in Port Whisper. It gave the locals comfort to have one of their own taking over as police chief, and Morgan didn't miss the sparkle of pride in his father's eyes.

Morgan had finally done it. He'd made Dad proud. Yet he hadn't wanted to move back in. Morgan needed to strike out on his own, be an adult in his own home, yet be close enough to help Dad when needed. So, Morgan had bought his own bungalow a few blocks away.

"Down the hall is the third bedroom, which Dad uses as an office, and the bathroom. It should be in pretty good shape, but I'll give it the once-over before we leave."

"Nonsense. Bathrooms are my specialty," Edith said.

"Where are you going to sleep?" Julie asked.

"The office. There's a sofa bed in there. I'll get your things from the truck." Morgan stepped around them, practically sprinting down the stairs.

What was the matter with him? He guessed the edginess was due to the reality of Julie being so close, living under the same roof, Morgan seeing her first thing in the morning, saying good-night before she went to his…her room.

The situation felt so surreal, and he suddenly questioned his decision to invite them to stay at his dad's. Was this just about protecting them, or did a part of Morgan have another motivation?

He grabbed two suitcases from the truck and started for the house.

"Hey, Chief!" Anderson Green called from his back porch next door. "Got company?"

"Yep, Edith Burns and her daughter, Julie. Edith's having some work done on her floors."

"Julie Burns, eh?" Anderson winked.

"She's just here for a visit. Don't start anything. The gossip mill is already full."

"Wouldn't dream of it."

"Have a good day."

"You, too."

Morgan headed up the stairs, imagining Anderson and his buddies at Wednesday coffee shooting the breeze, and Anderson dropping the bomb about two women moving in with the chief of police. But Morgan couldn't worry about appearances and idle gossip. His goal was to protect Julie and her mom, resolve this mess she'd been sucked into and send her back to Seattle.

*Keep your eye on the ball, buddy.*

As he got to the top of the stairs, the back door opened and Julie shared a wry smile. "Mom's already at work on the kitchen."

Morgan stepped inside to the frenzy of Edith cleaning out supplies beneath the sink.

"Mrs. Burns, you really don't need to—"

"Sure I do. I want to earn my stay, don't I? Besides, I love to clean."

Morgan glanced at Julie. "She does," Julie said. "Lana and I called it a CD—cleaning disorder."

"A clean house is the sign of a peaceful mind," Edith shot over her shoulder.

"I'll take these upstairs." He carried the suitcases up the stairs and deposited them in their respective rooms. Edith had her hands full by attacking the kitchen, so he'd take care of putting fresh sheets on the beds. Morgan opened the hall closet and pulled out a set of sheets for Dad's bed, and Morgan's.

Julie. Staying in Morgan's room. Surrounded by his personal trophies, which included keepsakes from their relationship: notes they'd shared in school, the silver cross she'd given him for his sixteenth birthday and the one photograph he couldn't bring himself to rip up—the photograph of Julie on Twanka Cliff gazing across Puget Sound.

*Snap out of it.* He needed to move this case forward and send her back to Seattle, not get dragged down into the past.

He shook his head and shut the closet door. Julie was standing there, holding out her hands. "Here, I'll help. It will go quicker."

He passed her a set of sheets. "Dad's bed" was all he could say.

With a smile, she took the sheets and disappeared into Dad's room. He figured he had just a few minutes to "Julie-proof" his room—hide whatever keepsakes he could find before she moved in.

The sound of humming echoed across the hall, a habit of Julie's since she was a kid. He found the photograph and silver cross and shoved them in the bottom drawer beneath some old clothes. The box of love notes was on the top shelf of the closet. There'd be no reason for her to go digging around up there, so he got to work on the bed.

As he stripped off the sheets, he remembered the many nights he'd lain here, holding the phone to his ear, whispering endearments to his high-school sweetheart.

A long time ago. He'd grown up, let go of the Julie dream and had moved on. Who was he kidding? If he'd moved on there wouldn't be a box of keepsakes in his closet.

Hovering in his room, picturing himself talking to her late at night, started an ache in his chest he most certainly didn't welcome, or need, right now.

She'd left because Morgan wasn't what she'd wanted; he wasn't good enough, period. He was no match against her goal of moving to the city and counseling kids, and probably finding some citified guy to fall in love with. And for the second time in his childhood—at eighteen, just as he was about to embark on the beginning of adulthood—Morgan had been abandoned.

He snapped the clean sheet over the mattress and made the bed, struggling to shelve his memories and get his pain in check. He'd need a clear head if he were going to keep Julie and her mom safe.

"Need help?" Julie said, leaning against the doorjamb.

"Nope, I'm good," he said, not looking up. He slipped a fresh case on the pillow and tossed it on the bed. "We'd better get to Seattle."

They went downstairs and Julie hesitated, turning to Morgan.

"Thanks again for helping us."

"It's my job," he said, hoping to convince himself that his job was his primary motivation.

"I know, but letting us move in here is really going above and beyond. I mean, we could have rented a room at the Port Whisper Inn or something."

"You're safer here, with me."

"You sure about that?"

"I may be a small-town cop, but I know my business, Julie."

"That's not what I—"

"Let's check on your mom." He brushed past her, needing to put space between them. How was he going to do that when they had to spend the next three hours in a car together?

"You okay in here, Edith?" Morgan said coming into the kitchen.

She wasn't alone. Caroline Ross was unloading boxes lined up on the counter.

"Hi, Chief. Thought I'd help stock the kitchen," Caroline said.

"Great idea," Julie said, walking around Morgan. "Mom thinks she's superwoman, but even superheroes need a partner."

Julie gave her mom a hug. "We have to get going."

Mom dried her hands on a checked towel Morgan didn't recognize, and held her daughter's hands. "I know this is going to be hard, sweetie. Keep the Lord in your heart and He'll see you through, okay?"

"Sure." Julie slipped her hands from her mom's and made for the back door.

Morgan wondered if Edith knew how much distance Julie had put between herself and God. Jules went out the back door and Morgan nodded at her mom.

"I'll take good care of her, Edith."

"I know you will. God bless, Morgan."

"Thanks."

*We're always right behind you.*

The mystery caller's threat echoed in Julie's head, over and over again, as they headed to the ferry. She caught herself checking the side-view mirror for the umpteenth time.

"It's okay. No one's following us," Morgan said, his eyes trained on the road ahead.

He was reading her mind again, sensing her trepidation. Was that a good thing or bad? She wasn't sure, and she really didn't know how to talk to him without setting him off. She'd tried to thank him for opening his father's home as a sanctuary, but Morgan took offense, assuming…what? From his reaction he assumed she was questioning his ability to protect her, being that he was nothing but a small-town cop.

That wasn't what she'd meant and she'd tried telling him so, but he'd shut her down. No, when she'd asked if he was sure about her being safer with him, what she really meant was that their close proximity could open up a plethora of emotional wounds sure to drive them both nuts. And make them question everything about the past ten years.

At least it would for Julie.

She fought back the self-questioning spiral. She was tired, that's all. After the challenge of pulling straight As in college, finding a job that would satisfy her need to do good work and then watching teens fail, no matter how hard she'd tried to save them, Julie was suddenly drained and vulnerable to so many things.

It would be too easy to fall into Morgan's arms again. But she wouldn't, she couldn't. She'd put him through enough and sensed he hadn't forgiven her for their breakup.

Guilt ripped through her chest. She closed her eyes. She'd done the right thing. She'd sacrificed their love so both she and Morgan could pursue their own dreams. It had been the honorable, mature thing to do, right?

*Don't fool yourself, Jules. It had less to do with honor and more to do with your desperate need for redemption.*

With a sigh, she fought back the niggling voice that had haunted her all these years.

"I picked up a new phone for you," Morgan said, interrupting her mental analysis.

"Great, thanks," she said. He actually instigated a conversation. That had to be good, right?

He handed her the phone. "Give the number to your family. I've programmed my number as speed dial 1. I've turned off the GPS so you can't be traced, except for 9-1-1 calls. Do you need anything from your apartment? More clothes, toiletries, anything like that?"

"I could use some warmer clothes."

"We'll stop by after we meet with Ethan."

"It's great that you keep in touch with him."

"Yep."

"Does he like his job with the Seattle P.D.?" she asked.

"Yep."

"I heard you were with King County Sheriff's police."

"I was."

"How'd you like that?"

"Fine."

So much for pleasant conversation. He was being civil, polite...detached.

Fine, she'd respect his method of self-preservation, even if it felt as if he was being rude.

They spent the next few hours in silence, guilt gnawing its way through her conscience: guilt for breaking Morgan's heart, guilt for not being able to save more runaway teens...

Guilt for not being there for Suzy when she'd needed Julie the most.

Because Julie had been with Morgan.

Boy, going back to Port Whisper last night had really messed with her head. She'd intellectually resolved her issues with Suzy's death, at least she thought she had. But Julie considered that somewhere, deep down, the guilt still fueled her every decision.

They arrived at the medical examiner's office in the Harborview Medical Center. Ethan Beck, a tall man with dark, cropped hair and sky-blue, eyes was waiting for them in the family lounge.

"Julie Burns, how are you?" Ethan extended his hand but Julie went in for a quick hug. Ethan had been a good influence on Morgan growing up, and she'd always be grateful to him.

"It's good to see you," she said. "Had I known

you were a Seattle cop I would have come to you instead of running to Port Whisper."

"What, and miss getting personal attention from a police chief?" he teased.

"Let's ID the body," Morgan said, irritation in his voice.

Ethan's expression hardened. "Why don't you have a seat in the family area. I'll get the photograph."

"You mean, I won't have to actually see the body?" Julie asked, slightly relieved.

"No, wait here. I'll get the medical examiner."

As Ethan went down a long, gray hallway, Julie couldn't help but remember Andy's mischievous smile and determined attitude. He was a fighter, and she thought he'd changed his battleground. She'd thought he was fighting for a healthier, productive life.

Yet now his body, a shell empty of spirit and personality, most likely lay on a cold slab down the hall.

Hugging herself, she released a sigh.

"Jules?" Morgan said.

She glanced at him.

"It'll be okay."

She bit back a frustrated retort. If she heard "It'll be okay" one more time, she was going to lose it and scream.

"Thanks," she said.

Ethan walked toward them accompanied by a middle-aged woman in a white lab coat. She carried something in her hand: the photograph.

Julie's pulse raced into her throat at the thought of what Andy would look like. They approached her and the woman offered a consoling smile. "He was beaten up pretty bad, but his face is identifiable. Are you ready?"

Julie nodded and Morgan put his arm around her for support. "You can do this."

And she could, as long as Morgan stayed close.

The medical examiner held up the photograph…

# Chapter Five

The air rushed from Julie's lungs.

She turned and buried her face against Morgan's chest. "It's not him."

Relief warred with sadness as the image of the dead boy's face seared into her brain. Bruised, broken, lifeless.

"It's okay," Morgan said, stroking her back. For a second the comforting gesture calmed her frantic heartbeat, then anger burned its way through her chest.

"It's not okay, Morgan. He's dead for no reason, and…and it's all so ridiculously senseless."

Julie walked away from the group and went outside.

"Jules," Morgan called after her.

She couldn't stop running, running from the image of death, the tragedy of a boy's life ending in such a violent way. Running from the frustration that she hadn't been able to save him.

Leaning against the cold cement wall just outside the door, she crossed her arms over her chest and fought back the sadness eating away at her.

"Jules?" Morgan touched her hair and she fought not to lean into his touch.

She glanced up at him. "I'm just so frustrated. I give everything I have to help these teenagers, I try to save them, point them in the right direction, and yet there's a dead boy in there and I couldn't do anything to prevent it and—"

"Hey, stop. You're making it sound like it's your job to save all of them. You didn't even know that kid."

"It doesn't make it any less frustrating." She faltered, glancing at the cement walkway. "To see him that way."

"True, but it's not your job to save the world, Jules. Talk about setting yourself up for failure. Come on, let's swing by your apartment."

With a nod, she stepped away from him, breaking contact. Although his touch seemed to calm her, she accepted the fact he was being polite, that's all. She didn't want to rely or depend on Morgan, or anyone else, for that matter. She'd learned years ago, after Dad died, that people you depended on could be taken away, which was why she'd developed a healthy sense of self-reliance.

As they headed for Morgan's truck in the parking lot, she refocused on Andy, stoking hope in her heart that he was still out there fighting his way back to safety.

"What's your address?" Morgan said, turning on the car.

"It's 109 John Street. It's by the Seattle Center."

"We should make it quick."

"You think someone's watching the apartment?"

"It's possible." He glanced at her and cracked a slight smile. "Nothing to worry about. You've got your trusty bodyguard."

She wanted to smile back, but couldn't focus past the image of the dead boy.

"How do you do that?" she said.

"What?"

"Smile after seeing something so horrible?"

"It's tragic, Jules, but death is a part of life. Besides, he's—"

"Don't say it."

"What?"

"That he's at peace with the Lord."

"But—"

"Let me ask you something." Jules squared off at him. "Where is God when these kids are fighting for their lives? When they're abandoned by their parents, who are supposed to love and care for them? When they're sleeping in the freezing cold under an overpass, or...or digging in garbage cans for food?"

"With good comes evil, Jules. You know that. It's not God's role to fix everything for us. Challenges make us stronger, and faith in God gives us the strength to be able to carry our burdens."

Julie shook her head and glanced out the front window. "He never listens to my prayers."

"He listens. You're just not getting the answers you're expecting."

"Whatever." She didn't want to talk about it anymore, argue or discuss God. It always frustrated her.

They headed past the Seattle Public Library and north on Fourth Avenue. Not wanting to be obvious that she was leaving for an extended period of time, Julie had packed light, stuffing her backpack with essentials, figuring she could buy clothes when she got to Port Whisper, or better yet, borrow from Lana.

"Do you know your neighbors?" Morgan asked.

"Not well. I leave early and get home past seven most nights."

"Long day."

"Says the guy who's on duty every day of his life."

"We have that in common," Morgan said.

"What?"

"Our jobs are also our vocations. You dedicate your life to teenagers and I dedicate mine to the citizens of Port Whisper. Of course, I know you probably think mine is a cakewalk compared to what you see every day, but you'd be surprised."

"What do you mean?"

"As the chief, and son of the previous chief, everyone looks up to me and confides in me. There's stress in being perfect all the time, stress in counseling people when I have no training in psychology. I hope I respond in a helpful way, either by offering advice, or just listening. But I never really know."

"How do you decide what to do?"

"I pray for guidance. I know you don't want to hear that, but God is the beacon of light as I navigate my way through life. When all else fails, I add the person to my daily prayer list."

"You pray every day?"

"First thing in the morning, right before breakfast. It energizes me, helps me focus on what's important." He glanced at her, then back to the cars ahead. "Guess that makes me a dork or something."

"No, I just don't remember you being so religious."

"Don't you remember us going to church together? Holding hands as we sang the hymns?"

She did, but didn't want to. She couldn't deal with the emotional pain of the past right now.

"I guess," she said.

"I sought God's light to help me cope with Dad's moods, to help me…" He faltered. "Get over you."

"Do you hear God when you pray to Him?"

"It's more like a feeling, a direction. I surrender myself in a given situation, and do what feels right in my heart. God is about love, after all."

They turned onto John Street.

"That's my building," she said.

"I'll park a few blocks away in case someone's watching. I don't want them to track us by getting my plate number."

"Oh, okay."

He pulled up to the curb and glanced at her. "When we get inside, stay behind me, okay?"

"Sure."

They walked side by side the two blocks to her building, Morgan continually scanning the street. Although her place was tucked away behind the Seattle Center, there was always plenty of foot traffic during big events.

"Hang on," Morgan said, stopping short about ten feet from the apartment building.

She peered around him. The front door was ajar.

"Sometimes we leave it open when we're moving stuff in and out," Julie offered. She didn't want to assume this was a nefarious sign related to her stalker.

"Just the same, let's take it slow." He edged his way toward the front door, just as one of Julie's neighbors wheeled a dolly stacked with boxes around the corner.

"Oh, hey," she called out to Julie.

"Hi, Heather." Julie's anxiety eased. "See," she said to Morgan. "She left it open."

"Did you connect with your uncle?" Heather asked.

"Pardon me?" Julie said. She didn't have an uncle.

"Your uncle stopped by this morning looking for you. He said you missed dinner last night and he was worried."

Morgan glanced at her, slightly shaking his head.

Julie got the message. "We must have just missed each other."

"Can I help with the door?" Morgan offered, holding the door for Heather.

"Thanks." She smiled at Morgan and a twang of jealousy shot through Julie. How silly. What right did she have to feel jealous about anything Morgan did? She studied him. Was he attracted to Heather? No, he was fixated on the stairs leading to Julie's apartment.

"See you guys later," Heather said, pressing the elevator button.

"'Bye." Julie started up the stairs, but Morgan gently grabbed her arm.

"Me first," he said.

"Right, sorry. I don't have an uncle," she whispered.

"I know."

"Do you think—"

"Probably. Let's focus on getting your clothes and getting back home."

*Home.* It had been a long time since she thought of Port Whisper as her home.

They got to the second floor and she pointed to her apartment. He opened his hand and she passed him her keys. "Stay flat against the wall. If something goes wrong, head down the back stairs to the restaurant next door and call 9-1-1."

"Okay."

"Under no circumstances do you come inside until I tell you it's safe to do so."

She nodded, fighting back another adrenaline rush.

Morgan stuck the key in the door and unlocked it, disappearing inside. The door didn't automatically shut, the charm of an old building. She listened intently for sounds of a struggle, or for Morgan's signal to join him. Seconds dragged like hours as she stood there, clutching the phone.

The front door to the building slammed closed down below. Footsteps echoed up the stairwell and she held her breath. What if her "uncle" had been waiting across the street for her to return home?

She peeked inside her apartment, unable to see anything but the long hallway leading to the living room.

Footsteps grew louder, closer…

The back of a man's head came into view and she jumped into her apartment and gently shut the door. Pressing her forehead against the aged wood, she took a slow, deep breath and eyed the peephole.

Nothing. It could be an upstairs neighbor, or a visiting family member.

She was overreacting. Heading into the living room, she framed her cheeks with her hands, trying to ground herself. She turned the corner into the living room and stopped short. Sofa cushions and pillows were scattered across the floor, the coffee table lay upside down like a dead animal and books had been ripped off her shelves and thrown haphazardly onto the ground. Her favorite afghan, the one Mom crocheted as a high-school graduation present, was crumpled on the floor instead of stretching proudly across the back of the sofa.

Then realization hit her: no Morgan.

She opened her new cell phone to call the police, her heart pounding in her chest. She was about to press Send when he climbed through her living-room window.

He stood and brushed his hands on his jeans. "I thought I told you to stay in the hallway."

"I got spooked. I saw some guy coming up the stairs and panicked that it was my long-lost uncle."

"Well, this is how they got in. Didn't bother to close the window all the way."

A knock at the door made her yelp.

Morgan put his finger to his lips and went to the door. He looked through the peephole, stepped aside and motioned for her to do the same. "You know him?"

She recognized William. "It's my friend from work. He's okay."

She swung open the door against Morgan's protest. "William?"

"Thank God you're okay. I was so worried after your phone call this morning."

"I'm fine, come in."

William stepped into her apartment and eyed Morgan.

"William Pratt, this is an old friend, Morgan Wright," she introduced.

Morgan reluctantly shook hands. Being a cop, it was natural to be suspicious of strangers, she figured. But William was kind and hardworking. At forty-six, he'd made it longer with these kids than anyone else at the office, and some days she wished she knew his secret—what kept him going with a smile on his face.

Morgan shut the door and locked it. She motioned William into the living room and Morgan followed.

"I tried your cell, but it went into voice mail. I was hoping I'd catch you before you disappeared." William glanced across the disheveled living room. "Whoa."

"Like I mentioned on the phone, someone's after me and I need to fly under the radar."

"I guess that means there's no way you'd come into the office?"

"No," Morgan answered.

Julie cracked an apologetic smile at William. "I'm not sure I can risk it."

"That's unfortunate. Dynacorp only wants to take a meeting to discuss the grant if you're the one making the presentation."

"That's ridiculous. You and Helen know the material better than any of us."

"True, and Helen was steaming when we she

heard about the request. But you put it together, Julie. It's your brainchild."

"What grant?" Morgan asked.

"Dynacorp is a pharmaceutical company that offers grants every year to nonprofits," Julie explained. "We applied, and our interview presentation is scheduled for two weeks from now."

"They moved it up to next week," William said.

"Why?"

"Something about an executive leaving the country on business."

"Sorry to interrupt," Morgan said. "But I need to get Julie out of the city."

"Of course. Julie, if you need anything…" William offered.

"Thanks."

"What do you want me to tell the boss?"

"I emailed her that I'm taking a family-emergency leave. But—" she glanced at Morgan, then back to William "—let's see how this stalker thing goes. With any luck, it will be over soon and I can make the Dynacorp meeting."

"I hope so."

"Here, I have a new cell number." She wrote it down on the back of a receipt and handed it to him. "Call me with updates, okay?"

"Sure." William turned to leave, but Morgan stopped him. "I think it would be safer if we all left together." Morgan glanced at Julie. "You've got three minutes to pack."

"But my place is a mess."

"Can't worry about that now, Jules. Go on."

She knew he was right, and trusted his instincts. Trying to block out the violent image of her trashed living room, she went into her bedroom and pulled a suitcase out of her closet. She cast a glance around the room and found it curious that they hadn't trashed it, as well. A relieved sigh escaped her lips. The thought of the intruders touching her things, her personal things…

She shook her head and shoved as much as she could into the suitcase, focusing on the essentials. Socks, underwear, jeans and sweaters. She glanced at her jewelry box, hesitated and opened the top, grabbing a few pairs of earrings.

Figuring her three minutes were up, she hurried down the hall to the living room to find Morgan righting her furniture, and William reshelving her books.

"I'm ready," she said.

But she wasn't. She'd miss her place, the smell of garlic drifting through her window from the Italian restaurant downstairs, eating whole-wheat muffins and drinking tea in her cozy kitchen nook. It was a small, utilitarian apartment, but it had been her home for the past four years. She'd decided to get a small, live tree this year, and invite people from work over for a Christmas brunch.

"Okay, let's go." Morgan motioned William and Julie to stay behind him.

"He seems to know what he's doing," William said, nodding at Morgan.

"He should. He's a cop."

Morgan's instincts were on red alert. The break-in indicated that not only did they want something, but he suspected they probably hadn't found it.

And they'd keep coming.

He fought back the panic at the thought of Julie being home when the intruders had broken in. But she wasn't. She was safe, in Port Whisper.

"Where are you staying?" William asked as they stepped outside.

"I—"

"It's better if you don't know," Morgan interrupted.

"If you think that's best."

"It is, for your own safety," Morgan clarified.

William and Julie hugged and Morgan found himself wanting to step between them, tell them to break it up. He was being ridiculous.

"Stay in touch," William said.

"I will."

William reached out to shake Morgan's hand.

"Take care of her," William said.

"I plan to."

With a nod, William turned and walked toward First Avenue North. Morgan reached for Julie's bag. "Here, let me."

She handed it to him and they headed for his truck.

"Jules, we have to figure out what they were looking for in your apartment."

"Maybe the files I took with me? I don't know what else it could be. I'm just glad Andy is—" She hesitated. "I was going to say I'm glad he's okay, but we don't really know that, do we?"

"At least we can hope he's alive."

Morgan put her bag in the trunk and scanned the area one last time.

"Since we're in Seattle, weren't you going to stop by and see your dad?" she asked.

He motioned for her to get into the car. Morgan hadn't thought about Dad these past twenty hours. His mind had been too focused on keeping Julie safe.

They pulled out and he considered her question. "I wasn't going to."

"But you're in the city. I'm sure he'd be glad to see you."

"Us. I'm not leaving you alone, Jules. You sure you're up to a hospital visit?"

"Of course. It's the right thing to do as long as we're here."

"We'll make it a quick one. Dad will understand."

Morgan headed to the hospital, wondering what Dad's reaction would be to Morgan walking in with Julie by his side. Dad had always liked Julie, that is, until she'd left Morgan. It brought all of Dad's resentment to the surface of being abandoned by his own wife. *She's a spoiled, self-centered female, just like your mother.* His bitter words hadn't helped Morgan heal from the betrayal. They had rekindled his anger. Over and over again.

Morgan fought back the memory. Had to redirect his train of thought.

"Tell me about that William guy," he asked.

"He's been with Teen Life for twenty years, can you believe that?"

"Dedicated man."

"And so good with the teenagers. But I think he's tired, burning out."

"Is he married?"

"Why do you ask?"

"Just curious."

"He's divorced, actually. I never really understood that. He's a very kind and gentle man."

"You two are close?" Morgan asked

"Where are you going with this?"

"Just making conversation."

"You're jealous," she said teasingly, a slight smile curling her lips.

"I have no right to be jealous of anything you do."

Her smile faded and she glanced out the side window. Had he hurt her feelings somehow? Why? He was only stating the truth.

They drove the rest of the way in silence, a good thing. Morgan needed to strategize how he was going to walk into Dad's room with Julie and avoid unnecessary tension. The last thing she needed was to be scolded by his father about a decision she'd made ten years ago.

A few minutes later they got to the hospital and went up to see his dad. Hesitating outside his room, Morgan said, "Give me a second with him first."

"Sure."

"Stay right here."

"I will."

Morgan went into the white, antiseptic room. Dad had his readers on the bridge of nose, deep into an article in *Time* magazine.

"Hey, Dad."

His dad snapped off his glasses. "Morgan, I didn't know you were stopping by."

"I was in the city on an assignment. How are you feeling?"

"Today's a B-minus day." He smiled.

Dad had mellowed in the past few years. Morgan was thankful for that, thankful that Dad had enjoyed a few years of fun before the cancer had struck.

"What kind of assignment? Maybe I could help."

"Actually," Morgan pulled a vinyl chair closer to the bed and sat down. "It involves an old friend, Julie Burns."

Dad's face hardened. "I don't understand. She left Port Whisper, what, ten years ago?"

"She came back. She's in trouble."

"Not your problem."

"I'm making it my problem."

"Don't be a fool, Morgan."

"I'm not a fool, I'm a cop. She's in danger and she came to Port Whisper for sanctuary."

"Well, she always was good at running, just like your mother."

Julie wandered into the room before Morgan could stop her.

"Hi, Chief Wright," she said, slowing as she got closer. "I was sorry to hear about your condition."

Dad's jaw hardened. "Thank you."

"So, Morgan took over as chief. That's exciting."

"And helpful to you, isn't it?" he said, pinning her with angry eyes.

"Dad," Morgan warned.

"What?" Dad snapped.

"Be nice."

"I'm all outta nice, especially for people who hurt my family."

"I'm sorry, I—"

"Save it," Dad interrupted her. "So you're back in Port Whisper to torture my son?"

"That's it." Morgan stood. "We'd better go."

"No." Julie touched his arm. "I don't want to ruin your time with your dad. I'll wait in the family area."

"No, you won't. I'm not letting you out of my sight."

"Come on, boy, don't fall for this again," Dad chided.

Morgan stepped up to the end of his father's bed. "Please stop being rude. The past is the past. Julie's in trouble and I won't abandon her, and risk her being hurt, or worse."

"She abandoned you without a second thought."

"I've moved on," Morgan said. "This is a professional relationship. Now, are you going to let go of the past or should we leave?"

Dad narrowed his eyes and studied Julie. Morgan could sense her start to edge out of the room. He reached out and held her hand to keep her close.

"What kind of trouble is she in?" Dad asked.

"Someone's after her. She works with streets kids and witnessed one of them being kidnapped. She's been getting threatening calls and her office was broken into. We just stopped by her apartment and it was ransacked."

"You think it's related to her work?" Dad asked Morgan.

Morgan figured it was easier for Dad to avoid looking at Julie. It brought back too many bad memories.

"Yes, sir, it looks that way," Morgan said. "She doesn't have much of a life outside of her job."

"Gee, thanks," Julie muttered.

"Am I lying?" Morgan said.

"Nope. Work consumes my life."

"You think someone's after her because she witnessed the kidnapping?" Dad pressed.

"Perhaps, but if that's the case, why break into her office and her apartment? They thoroughly searched her place."

Dad, back in cop mode, leveled Julie with intense eyes. "You know what they're after?"

"Haven't a clue."

"Did they take anything from your apartment?"

"Not that I could tell." She glanced at Morgan. "We didn't have time to look around."

"I wanted to get out of there, in case someone was watching the place."

"She lives in Seattle," his dad said. "The Seattle P.D. should be handling this."

"I'm working with my buddy Ethan Beck. He's a detective with the Seattle P.D. Dad—" Morgan paused. "Julie has moved back to Port Whisper temporarily and, well… I've invited her and her mom to stay in your house until this is resolved."

Morgan held his breath, hoping his dad didn't flip out in front of Julie.

"Is Edith in danger, too?" Dad asked.

Dad had always liked Edith Burns.

"Julie got a threatening call and we didn't want to risk her being tracked to the Burnses' home. So yeah, both of them are moving in. In retrospect, I guess I should have asked first, but I figured they could help me spruce up the place, and my house is too small for guests."

"And the neighbors will keep an eye on things," Dad added. "How long will she be staying in Port Whisper?"

"We don't know yet. Until the case is resolved and it's safe for her to return to Seattle."

And she would, Morgan reminded himself. Although his dad feared Morgan would fall back into love with Julie, there was no chance of Morgan letting that happen. He recognized this situation for what it was: temporary.

They chatted for a few minutes. Morgan filled Dad in on the happenings in town, and Dad shared frustrations about his condition. Julie smiled and nodded when appropriate, but didn't say much. She probably sensed it was safer to remain quiet than give Morgan's Dad something to snap at her about.

"I'll check back in a few days," Morgan said.

"I'll be here."

"Good to see you again, Chief," Julie offered.

Dad offered a curt nod and went back to his article.

"Mom said they'll have dinner ready when we get there," Julie told Morgan, pocketing the phone.

"Sounds good."

That was about all they said during the rest of the trip back to Port Whisper. Morgan sensed she felt bad about Dad's verbal assault, but he didn't know quite what to say, how to apologize. Truth was, Dad needed to move on.

And so did Morgan.

*How do I do it, Lord? How do I let go of this buried resentment?*

He remembered Colossians 3:13: "Bear with each other and forgive whatever grievances you may have against one another. Forgive as the Lord forgave you."

Wasn't it about time Morgan forgave Julie with his whole heart?

*Focus on the case, not the past.* Morgan lost count how many times he'd repeated this in his head over the past twenty-four hours. He'd keep repeating it until he was sure the past wouldn't mess with his head and prevent him from keeping Julie safe.

He glanced across the front seat at his passenger. Julie's face was tipped toward her side window, her eyes closed. He eyed the road, but that sweet image of her delicate features—her perfectly shaped nose, full lips and flawless skin—lingered in his mind.

She was just the way he remembered her, only when he'd dreamed of her against his will, she smiled more and her golden eyes sparkled when Morgan cracked a joke.

That sparkle was absent, at least he hadn't seen a glimpse of it since they ran into each other yesterday. Had her job totally sucked that loving, hopeful energy from her? She seemed determined to help the teenagers survive the brutal streets, yet it was as if she expected them to fail.

She'd lost her faith, and Morgan wondered if it was God's plan to bring them back together after ten years so Morgan could help her find her way back.

Her cell rang and she quickly grabbed it. So she wasn't asleep after all.

"Hello? Hey, Mom. We're just coming into town. Sure…okay. Love you, too."

Julie closed the flip phone. "Mom asked if we could stop by the house. Lana's picking up some things, but Mom forgot to tell her to get the fruit so it won't go bad."

"Lana shouldn't have gone to the house by herself."

"I'd like to see you try to tell Lana that. She's one determined cookie."

"Kind of like her sister." He meant it as a compliment. Julie looked away, and he could tell she didn't interpret it that way. In that moment he wondered who was emotionally beating her up more: Morgan or Julie?

They pulled onto her quiet street and turned into the driveway. Julie reached for her door, just as Morgan spotted movement by the side of the house.

"Hang on," he said, placing his hand on her arm.

"What's wrong?"

He didn't answer, hyper-focused on the side of the house. The moon cast an eerie glow across the property, giving off enough light to see...

A shadowy figure peering through the dining-room window.

# Chapter Six

"You don't think they—"

"Stay here," Morgan ordered.

He got out of the truck and closed the door, quietly. Stalking the perimeter of the property, he pulled out his firearm and came up behind the Peeping Tom.

"Police, don't move."

"Don't shoot!" a voice cracked. A teenage voice.

"Hands where I can see them."

The intruder raised his hands. "I didn't do anything."

"Turn around, slowly," Morgan ordered, adrenaline rushing through his veins.

The kid turned around and Morgan instantly recognized him: Caroline Ross's grandson Sketch.

Morgan holstered his gun. "What are you doing here?"

"I... She's inside and I wanted to talk to her," he said, his hands still reaching for the sky.

"Put your arms down."

Sketch slowly did as ordered.

"It's dangerous to be here, kid. Who's inside that you want to see? Lana?"

"No, Ashley. She texted me that she was helping Lana grab some stuff."

Morgan glanced at the truck and waved Julie over, then redirected his attention to Sketch. "Why didn't you just ring the doorbell?"

"I didn't think she'd let me in."

"Why not?"

"We had a—" he shifted from one foot to the other "—disagreement."

"Who's this?" Julie said, walking up to Morgan.

"Sketch, Caroline's grandson. Sketch, this is Lana's sister, Julie."

"You're her? The one Lana talks about all the time?" Sketch said.

"Well, I'm her only sister."

Morgan glanced across the property, still tense from the potential threat. "Let's get inside."

Julie and Sketch walked ahead as Morgan

stayed back and scanned the property for any signs of trouble.

Julie let herself in with the key and called out, "Lana?"

"Hey," Lana said, popping her head out of the kitchen. "What are you doing here?"

"Mom wanted to remind you to get the fruit."

"Oh, okay. We're almost done packing up a few things. Oh, hey, Sketch. You here to help?"

"I found him lurking outside," Morgan said.

Lana went up to Sketch and put her arm around his shoulder. "You never have to lurk, buddy. Come on, Ashley's in the kitchen."

"I'd better go." Sketch looked unsure and anxious, a lot like Morgan had been when he'd first asked Julie out.

Morgan fought back the memory.

"You're here, don't waste the opportunity to make things right," Morgan said.

On cue, Ashley came out of the kitchen. "Lana, I..." she glanced at Sketch. "Oh, hi."

Awkward silence filled the room.

"Julie, this is my part-time assistant, Ashley," Lana introduced.

"Nice to meet you." Julie shook the girl's hand.

"Let's get everything together and head back to Dad's house," Morgan prompted.

Ten minutes later his truck was packed with

supplies from food to special blankets to fiction novels. Morgan eyed the novels, mostly cozy mysteries.

"Mom said since she wasn't sure how long she'd be staying at your house she wanted to make sure she and Julie had something to entertain themselves," Lana explained as Morgan shut the hatch to the trunk. "Although I don't know when she'll have time to read. She's got big plans for your dad's house."

"So, about the Christmas dance..." Sketch said to Ashley, shoving his hands into his pockets. "Do you, I mean, would you..."

"Just ask her already," Morgan said.

Julie slugged him in the shoulder.

"What?" Morgan said.

"Sure," Ashley said to Sketch.

He glanced at her, his face lighting up. "Cool."

"Hate to break this up, but we really have to go," Morgan said.

Ashley skipped to Lana's car and glanced over her shoulder at Sketch. She cracked a smile and the kid grinned.

"I'll text you," Sketch called.

"Meet you at the house," Lana said to Julie and Morgan.

As she and Ashley pulled out, Sketch fisted his hand. "Yes!"

A smile creased Julie's lips.

"Can we drop you off?" Morgan offered, opening the passenger car door for Julie. She climbed into the front seat.

"Nah, I'm pumped. I'm gonna walk."

"Good night, then." He shut Julie's door and Sketch blocked him.

"She's in trouble, isn't she?" He nodded at the car.

"That's police business."

Sketch waved him off. "Lana told Ashley what's going on and Ashley told me. I can help. I helped Jake, remember?"

"Thanks, kid, but I got this handled."

"If you change your mind, my email is sketch@cybermonkey.com. Need me to write it down?"

"I can remember, thanks."

"Cool." Sketch took off, practically dancing down the street.

Ah, young love. If Sketch only knew what was coming next.

Morgan shook it off and got in the car.

"They make a cute couple," Julie said.

Morgan didn't respond, remembering how the town referred to Morgan and Julie as a cute couple, the couple mostly likely to…

He stopped himself. If he really wanted to let go of the past, protect Julie and help her find her way back to God, he had to release his re-sentment. Completely.

*I can do it, Lord. With Your help, I know I can.*

Julie woke up tired and anxious the next day. Not because of an uncomfortable bed or a spicy meal. The emotional turmoil of the past day and a half had gotten to her.

Last night, seated at Morgan's Dad's kitchen table, she, Morgan, Mom and Lana had dined on an exceptional home-cooked meal of pot roast with potatoes, freshly baked biscuits, fruit and apple-crumb delight for dessert. Julie had for-gotten what it was like to enjoy a home-cooked meal. Most of her dinners consisted of popping a frozen dinner into the microwave and eating in front of the television at 8:00 p.m.

It felt good to be surrounded by family, to enjoy delicious food and easy conversation. Too good.

Halfway through the meal, an ache had started low in Julie's chest. Sadness. Regret.

Which had only worsened when she spent the night in Morgan's room, in Morgan's childhood bed. She had lain awake for hours, scanning his room, moonlight illuminating the rock-band posters and sport-hero figurines. Thinking the chill in the air prevented her from falling asleep, she got up and searched Morgan's closet. In her effort to grab a blanket off the top shelf, a shoe box fell, littering the floor with photographs, notes and dried leaves: keepsakes from Morgan and Julie's dating days.

Guilt warred with interest as she carefully plucked the keepsakes off the floor and placed them gently back into the box. She couldn't believe he'd kept them all these years, nor could she believe the emotions they stirred in her heart.

She'd felt such passion once, for Morgan, for God.

But now, some days, she felt, well, empty.

She got up and made the bed, reminding herself that as a counselor she had to develop skills to separate herself emotionally from the kids she counseled or she'd go nuts.

But had she separated so much of herself that she no longer felt anything? Had she hardened her heart to the point where she'd closed herself off to joy and love?

"Can't think about that now," she whispered.

She cracked open the bedroom door and heard her mom humming downstairs. Julie grabbed her things, showered and dressed. She applied mascara and blush, telling herself it had nothing to do with potentially seeing Morgan when she got downstairs.

What would this day bring? Hopefully nothing dangerous. Morgan assured her they weren't followed from Seattle, and she'd dumped her cell phone, destroying the GPS chip, right after she got the threatening call yesterday. Still, it wouldn't be that hard for someone to figure out where she'd grown up, and that she'd head back here to seek help from her family.

"Snap out of it," she coached. It did no good to fret. Besides, Morgan was in charge of the protection detail. He'd make sure she and Mom were safe.

A sense of peace washed over her. Relying on Morgan, depending on him was starting to feel…right. Comfortable.

Not good.

She came downstairs and followed the sound of Mom's humming, and the smell of freshly baked pastries.

"Hey, Mom," Julie said, coming into the kitchen.

"Good morning, sweetie. I made scones. Caroline's recipe."

"She actually shared it with you?" Julie teased, sitting at the table.

"Of course. You know Caroline. She figured her cranberry-nut scones could solve any problem. Tea?"

"Sure."

Mom poured a cup and placed it in front of Julie. "How did you sleep?"

"Okay, I guess."

Mom placed her hand on Julie's shoulder. "Worried about the case?"

"That, and other things." Julie glanced out the back window for Morgan's truck.

"He's at work, moving a few things around to clear his schedule," Mom said, reading Julie's thoughts.

"Why is he clearing his schedule?"

"He wants to be available for you."

Julie sighed. "I really didn't want to put him out."

"He doesn't see it that way."

"I'll bet he does."

"Here, have a scone." Her mom placed a warm scone on a plate and passed it to Julie. "Doesn't even need butter."

"Thanks."

The back door burst open and Lana raced into the kitchen, out of breath.

"What's wrong?" Julie said, suddenly tense.

"Chris called in sick and Ashley doesn't get out of school until 1:30 and I've got a tour scheduled to go out at ten to Sahalish Island." Lana collapsed in a chair at the kitchen table. "I mean, I've run the tours alone before, but I'd prefer not to, especially because we're serving cider and donuts. Multitasking is not my strength, as you guys know."

"I could help," Mom offered.

"No." Lana waved her off. "You said you thought you were getting a cold last night. You can't be out in this chilly weather for two hours."

"What about me?" Julie asked.

"I don't think Morgan would approve," Mom offered, sliding a scone in front of Lana.

"He doesn't control my life, Mom."

"You'd be great." Lana smiled at Julie.

"You should call Morgan first and ask," Mom warned.

"He put his number in my new phone." Julie called Morgan and he picked up on the first ring.

"Julie? Everything okay?"

"Yep, we're all fine, but Lana's in a pickle. She needs me to help with the tour to Sahalish Island today."

"No."

"Morgan—"

"You're safer at the house."

"These are tourists, Morgan. I'll be fine. And if I stay in this house twenty-four-seven, I'll go insane."

There was a pregnant pause and she worried that she'd offended him. "I mean, because I'm used to being out all the time, not because of the house or anything," she clarified.

"What time is the tour?"

"Ten."

"I'll meet you at the dock."

"No, you don't have to—"

"Jules, this is not up for negotiation."

"Okay, we'll see you there." Jules glanced at Lana. "He's joining us for the tour."

"Oh, he is, is he?" Lana winked at Mom.

"It's nothing like that."

Lana broke off a piece of her scone. "Uh-huh."


It was unusually nice weather for December in Port Whisper. As the tourists boarded Lana's boat, fondly called *Princess* and decked out in cheerful green, red and white lights for Christmas, Julie tipped her chin to take in the warmth of the bright sun. In those few seconds, she shut out the image of her trashed apartment and locked up her fear that she'd put her family in danger by coming to Port Whisper.

*Morgan will protect us.*

Was it fair to expect him to? She could see it in his eyes, his surrender of resentment toward her, and she feared what it could lead to: more heartbreak.

When this was over she planned to head back to Seattle and her job, more late nights and her nonexistent social life. That was okay with her, truly, if it meant she kept one more teenager alive and showed him a future of possibilities.

Someone bumped her and her eyes popped open.

"Sorry, sorry," a middle-aged man said, stepping onto the boat.

"It's okay," she responded with a smile.

She should have been paying attention anyway. How could she keep herself safe if she was spacing out?

The dozen tourists filed on board and Julie glanced across the street for Morgan. Worry set her on edge. He said he'd be here.

"Is Morgan coming?" Lana said.

"He said he was."

"We can wait a bit."

"I don't want to put your business in jeopardy."

"Another few minutes won't hurt. I'll start the introductions." Lana breezed up to the front of the boat and addressed the tourists. "I'm Lana Burns and that's my sister, Julie. Before we get started we should go over a few rules. First, everyone wears a flotation device. You can locate them under your seats."

The tourists, ranging in age from twenty-five to seventy-five, pulled out the royal-blue flotation devices and put them on. Lana tossed Julie a flotation device and Julie hesitated before putting it on, brushing her hand across the rough nylon.

Would Suzy have survived if she'd been wearing one?

"Jules?" Morgan said, walking up behind her.

Slightly disoriented by the memory of her childhood friend, Julie said, "You're late."

Morgan eyed her, probably sensing something was off. Julie turned to Lana. "Morgan needs one."

Lana tossed Morgan a flotation device and went back to her introductions. "We have a special guest with us today, our esteemed police chief, Morgan Wright."

Morgan gave a cursory wave and the tourists looked impressed.

"Better make sure it's tight," Morgan said, securing the buckle on Julie's vest.

Her gaze drifted up to meet his eyes, a warmer shade of blue than usual. It must be the sun, she thought. His eyes tended to change color in the sun. Their color had always captivated her, especially when she was young and in love. Those eyes, their love, had caused her to turn her back on her friend when she'd needed her most.

"What is it?" Morgan said, touching her jacket sleeve.

"Nothing." She snapped her gaze to Lana,

who was in the midst of explaining the day's schedule and refreshments.

"Jules?" Morgan pressed.

"Let's sit down." Julie headed for a spot in the back and Morgan followed.

"Hang on, Chief," Lana said. "I'm putting you to work today. Can you cast us off?"

"Sure thing."

Morgan uncoiled the rope from the dock, and Lana turned to steer the boat. Headset in place, she gave a brief history of Port Whisper as she pulled away from the dock. "By the late 1800s, Port Whisper was a well-known seaport, which is why much of our original architecture is ornate Victorian."

As she continued her lecture, Morgan made his way to the back and shifted beside Julie. It was close quarters and their legs touched; they couldn't *not* touch. She didn't want to pull away and hurt his feelings. But that wasn't the real reason she didn't shift away from him. She felt grounded by the connection, the pressure of his solid thigh against hers.

She glanced in the opposite direction, toward Canada. This was going to be a long day.

Luckily Lana put Julie to work the minute they docked at Sahalish Island. Julie served warm cider and cookies while Lana finished up the lecture on the island itself.

Morgan, Julie noticed, stayed on the fringes, cataloging every person who passed, assessing, analyzing. Would he be like this if Julie wasn't in trouble? She doubted it. She sensed he was usually a friendly, charismatic guy, especially with visitors to Port Whisper. She caught glimpses of that charm every now and then with this group.

"Take twenty minutes to walk around, check out the trails and views," Lana said. "But please don't wander past that bank of trees over there." She pointed. "Or the boulders along the perimeter there."

As the group broke up to take in the sights, a few women crowded Lana and Morgan with questions. Lana was really in her element, the center of attention, so outgoing and confident. And so different from the girl Julie grew up with. Lana had been the shy, awkward one living in Julie's shadow. Then, after Dad died, she'd grown depressed. Mom and Julie had worried that she'd never come out of it, that the darkness would pull her so far down that she wouldn't be able to see the light.

Like Suzy.

Julie bagged the trash and headed for a trail along the water. She'd gone ten years without feeling the shame of letting down her friend. She thought she'd moved past it, accepted the tragedy as not her fault, but the rather sad circumstance of a teenage girl drifting into depression. Julie had encouraged Suzy to speak with their pastor, but Suzy's mom didn't want anyone knowing their family's business: Suzy's dad was a verbally abusive alcoholic, and her mom just sat by and watched.

Then, when her boyfriend broke up with her and Suzy called Julie to throw her a lifeline… Julie had been unavailable.

Suzy had taken a boat out on her own, a small boat that couldn't handle the rocky waters caused by a wicked north wind. They'd ruled her death an accident, but in her heart Julie knew it could have been prevented, and it was partially Julie's fault.

Hugging her midsection, she walked up the trail as a flood of emotions bubbled up in her chest. Remorse. Regret. Shame.

Sudden rustling from the surrounding trees sent shivers up her spine. Was someone watching her? No, that was impossible. She was on an uninhabited island surrounded by tourists. Nothing could happen to her here.

Still, she turned and headed back toward the boat. Squinting to see into the distance, she realized she'd been so absorbed in thought she'd wandered out of view of the group.

Motoring back to the boat, she cast a nervous glance over her shoulder, fighting back the panic crawling down her spine. A sharp snap echoed from the bordering evergreens. She picked up her pace, desperate to get back to safety. What had she been thinking wandering off so far?

She hadn't been thinking. She'd been swallowed by the past, by the guilt she'd never released.

Guilt. Fear. Panic. The emotions clustered in her chest, making her break into a sprint. She shot another glance over her shoulder and tripped, stumbled and went down, bracing herself with her hand. She hit the ground and the air rushed from her lungs.

"Jules!" Morgan jogged up to her and helped her stand. "What happened?"

"I tripped."

"Jules?" With a bent forefinger, he tipped her face to look into his eyes.

"I thought someone was following me. Ridiculous, right?"

"What made you think that?"

"I heard something in the trees."

Squinting against the sun, Morgan scanned the area behind her.

"Locals do come out here to fish," he offered.

Just then, the sound of a boat's motor echoed from the other side of the trees.

"See?" Morgan said. "Probably just a fishing group."

As he steadied her with a hand to her arm, he said, "Why did you run off like that?"

"I didn't realize I'd gone so far. I was deep in thought."

"Thinking about…?"

She took a breath and looked him straight on. "It's my fault, Morgan. I'm responsible for Suzy's death."

"Don't talk like that."

"If I'd gone to see her when she'd called, she'd be alive today. But I didn't. I had to spend every waking moment with my boyfriend, and when she needed me most I was absent. I abandon the people I love. I did the same thing to you and Lana when I left. What kind of person am I? If only I had gone over there—"

"Jules, stop. Suzy's death was an accident."

"We don't know that for sure. But if I'd gone to her house that night she wouldn't have taken the boat out by herself. She wouldn't have—"

Morgan pulled her to his chest. "Shh. Don't do this to yourself. That's a heavy load you've been carrying, sweetheart. And it's unnecessary."

She leaned back and looked into his eyes.

"What kind of person abandons the people she loves? What is the matter with me?"

"You didn't abandon those boys, Andy and Dane, even though caring about them put you in danger."

"Great, I stick by strangers over the people closest to me."

"Look, Suzy did what she was going to do regardless of whether you went to her that night or not. You couldn't control her decision any more than I could control yours to leave Port Whisper."

"But—"

"Do you blame yourself for every runaway who walks through your door? Are you responsible for their choices?"

"No, I guess not."

"But a part of you thinks you are."

Julie shrugged.

"You felt guilty about Suzy so you chose a profession where you could save kids. I get that. But, Jules, at some point the people you love or the kids you counsel have to make their own decisions, they have to have faith in themselves and God for a better life. Suzy's parents should have been there for her first and foremost, then her pastor, friends and neighbors. Her death was not your fault."

"It feels like it."

"You're holding on to a lot of guilt that isn't deserved. I'd suggest praying to God for forgiveness, but I suspect this is more about you forgiving yourself."

The thought of forgiving herself had never entered her mind.

"We'd better go." As he led her up the trail to the boat, her cell phone rang.

"Hello?" she answered.

Silence. Her heart slammed against her chest. Was it another threatening call?

"Hello?" she tried again, glancing at Morgan.

"Miss Burns, it's Andy."

## Chapter Seven

Andy, the first missing boy. Julie's heart leaped into her throat.

"Andy? How did you get this number?" she asked.

"I got it from Mr. Pratt. He said you've been looking for me."

"I've been worried. You disappeared and—"

"I'm fine. Where are you?"

"I'm visiting friends."

"Where, in Seattle?"

"Andy, what's wrong? You sound upset."

"I said I'm fine," he croaked. "Are you coming back?"

"Eventually, but—"

"Here's Mr. Pratt."

A few seconds passed.

"I thought you'd feel better if you heard from Andy," William said.

"Is he okay?"

"Seems good to me. I've got him set up to stay in a halfway house tonight."

"But he was missing for a week. Did he say where he was, what happened?"

William hesitated. "He's not saying much. I don't want to press and have him disappear again."

"True. William, thank you so much for having him call."

"Sure thing. You take care."

"You, too."

Julie ended the call and glanced up into Morgan's amazing eyes.

"It was Andy. He's okay."

"Then what's bothering you?" he asked as they rejoined the group.

"Something in his voice sounded off. He asked where I was and when I'm coming back. I'm worried, Morgan."

"One thing at a time. Let's get back to town and go over your files again. The sooner we puzzle through this, the sooner you'll be safe, and be able to return to Seattle and your kids."

As she sat across the desk from him, Morgan sensed Julie was a tangle of nerves. She'd been spooked on the island and he'd managed to calm her down. Yet he couldn't take any chances, and asked Deputy Chief Scott Finnegan to go through fishing permits to see if he could track down who was driving the motorboat they'd heard.

Morgan doubted her stalker would go to the trouble of renting a boat and following her out there on the off chance he'd get her alone. Yet by wandering off she'd been isolated, making herself an easier target than when she was surrounded by family and friends in Port Whisper.

She wasn't thinking clearly, thanks to the ghosts of her past. Morgan wished he could say the right words to help her release the guilt about Suzy, but he knew that kind of absolution had to come from inside a person's heart.

One thing was for sure, her raw emotions triggered by the past were affecting her judgment. Which meant he'd have to think for the both of them in order to keep her safe.

An image of what could have happened on the island if it had, in fact, been her stalker, flashed across his mind. When he'd found her she'd been completely vulnerable, lying on the ground looking...

Dead.

His adrenaline had spiked big-time when he'd first caught sight of her motionless body.

Morgan rolled his neck and refocused on the papers in front of him. Did no good to go to that dark place again. As long as Julie was either at Dad's house or surrounded by people, Morgan was pretty sure she'd be okay. Besides, there was no evidence that her stalker knew she'd temporarily relocated to Port Whisper. As long as they kept her location a secret, they were good.

"What are we looking for?" she asked.

"Connections to anything unusual or dangerous. Tell me about Dane, the boy who was abducted. What was his family like? Does he have any brothers? What's his background in general?"

"High-school dropout, but a very smart boy. I encouraged him to get his GED, but no luck so far."

"Parents? Siblings?"

"Two brothers, younger, in foster care. His dad lost his job due to his drinking, and he's been in and out of jail for minor stuff. His mom abandoned them when Dane was twelve." Julie's gaze shot up to meet Morgan's. "Sorry."

"For what?"

"His mom, your mom. I mean, if it brings back bad memories."

"I've moved on, Jules. I won't lie, Mom's leaving affected my entire life, but it's pointless to hold on to the anger."

She glanced back at her paperwork. "Lecture alert."

"I wouldn't dare. I remember how I hated lectures when we were kids."

Julie snapped her eyes up to meet his. "But we're not kids anymore, are we?"

It felt as if she'd punched him in the gut. She never missed a chance to remind him that their past was way behind them and it was irrelevant to the present.

Too bad, she'd never convince him. Her life choices were born from events of her past, as were Morgan's. You couldn't deny the past; you had to learn from it. Somehow he'd make her understand that.

As he strategized ways to soften her to the idea, he realized she was still staring at him with those golden eyes. He fought the urge to reach out and place his hand over hers, comfort her, let her know it would all be okay.

And that he'd forgiven her.

He snapped his gaze from hers and refocused on the folder in front of him. A part of him still didn't want to forgive, but rather hold on to the fire of resentment, if for no other reason than to protect himself from what this woman could do to him…again.

But she could only hurt him if he gave in to the dream of them getting back together and living happily ever after in Port Whisper. That was not even close to any kind of reality. He pushed the thought aside, and realized he needed to move on by whatever means possible. *Yeah, how are you going to do that when she's living under the same roof?*

"Did you find something?" she asked, eyeing him.

His inner turmoil must be showing on his face. "Nope, just need more coffee." He got up and refilled his mug. "Can I get you some?"

"No, I'm good."

And she was. Still beautiful, smart and perfect in every way.

*Snap out of it, Wright.*

"What about Andy, the boy who went missing? What's he like?" Morgan asked.

"He's guarded, tough." She glanced at him. "Reminds me of you when you were his age."

"Getting into trouble, yeah, that sounds like me."

"No, I meant all that other stuff—how you made me laugh, how you acted like nothing bothered you, when I knew it did. Andy does that, too. He acts like everything's okay when I know it's not."

"Probably has to if he lives on the streets."

"Yeah, but he has a gentle side." She fingered

her silver locket. "He gave me this, even showed me the receipt to prove he didn't steal it."

Morgan eyed the gift, a silver butterfly locket.

"What pictures do you have inside?" He couldn't help asking.

"Actually, it doesn't open, but that's okay. The fact he used money he earned doing cleanup for the city means a lot to me."

"He appreciates what you've done for him." Morgan settled behind his desk.

"Yeah, well, it wasn't easy at first. He was rude and cynical. I didn't take it personally, but after months of his attitude I'd finally had it and called him out. That was a big turning point. He looked at me differently after that, with more respect, I guess."

"He learned you weren't a pushover."

"Yep, and I didn't let him get away with excuses. I helped Andy and Dane find temporary work doing festival cleanup, and Dane got a job at a pizza place. There was real hope for him."

"*Is,* Julie. There still *is* hope for him."

"I guess. He's strong and resilient. He could be okay."

Although she said the words, Morgan suspected she had little faith in their truth.

"Did Andy and Dane know each other? We should have asked Andy if he'd heard from Dane."

"They were friends, but I sensed they drifted apart when Dane got the job at the pizza place. Andy, well, he never saw much value in getting a regular job. He covers pretty well, but I sense he suffers from low self-esteem."

"Which makes him a prime candidate for drug abuse." Morgan tapped his pen to the folder on his desk. "What was Dane into?"

"He was working on kicking his meth habit. He was really determined."

"Did he ever deal?"

"I don't think so. Where are you going with this?"

"We have to assume his abduction had something to do with the drug culture. If he was a dealer, he had to get the drugs from somewhere and perhaps he was skimming off the top."

"No, I told you he had a real job."

"Jules, real jobs don't pay as well as dealing drugs."

"He was coming clean, completely. He wanted a stable life, wanted to go back to school, get married, have children…" Her voice trailed off and she glanced absently out the office window.

This line of questioning was upsetting her, so he backed off, closed his file and stood. "How about I take you back to the house? I've got some other police business I need to deal with. We can pick this up later."

"Okay, sure. I'm sorry if I'm taking you away from real work."

"This case is real work."

"I know, but I'm not even a resident of Port Whisper."

Morgan's desk phone rang and he grabbed it. "Chief Wright."

"I'll never get used to hearing those two words together," Ethan joked.

"Is that jealousy I hear in your voice?"

"More like respect. I see what our chief of D's goes through on a regular basis. I couldn't do it. Listen, we got a lead on Dane Simms. Someone thought they spotted a boy fitting his description last night in Denny Park."

"Doing what?" Morgan glanced at Jules.

"Running. That's why the ID is questionable. But the kid was wearing the coat and baseball cap Julie described and was about his height and weight. Someone called 9-1-1 but he eluded the patrolmen. Thought you should know."

"So he's alive, too."

"Too?"

"The first missing boy, Andy, called Julie this morning from the Teen Life office. Said he was okay, but Julie sensed something was off."

"She might have to reevaluate if she's over-reacting about these kids."

"That doesn't explain someone breaking into her office, and the threatening calls."

"I'm just saying, it's possible they're not related and your girlfriend might be into something she hasn't told you about."

"She's not… Never mind. Keep me posted. Thanks for calling, E."

"Think about it."

Morgan hung up and led Julie to the door.

"You're upset," she said. "What did he say?"

"They think they spotted Dane running through Denny Park last night."

"Running? From what?"

"Not sure. Could he have been high and freaking out?"

"No, I told you, he was clean. What else did Ethan say?"

He opened the door for her and they went outside. "That Dane's abduction might have nothing to do with whoever's stalking you." Morgan placed his hands on her shoulders. "Is there anything you haven't told me, anything at all?"

"Like what? Something illegal?"

"No, that's not what I'm asking."

"But the thought crossed your mind. Really, Morgan? You know me better than that."

"Ethan doesn't. He's asking the question."

"Is he? You sure?"

"Jules, we need to explore all options here.

Did you make someone angry or let someone down?"

"I live a pretty dull life, Morgan. Every day I fight an uphill battle to help street kids, I go home, eat and sleep. Then it all starts again."

"Who would benefit from you being out of the picture?"

"No one. I mean, I guess a few of the junior counselors, if they wanted to move up in the food chain, but honestly, Morgan, the money's not worth hurting me over."

"Someone's trying to scare you away. You having problems with anyone at work?"

She rubbed her forefinger and thumb against her locket. It appeared to be a touchstone, something to ground her. He wished he'd given it to her.

"Well, there's Helen but no, she's all bark and no bite."

"Last name?"

"Sutter."

He pulled a notebook from his pocket and wrote it down. "Do you know where she lives?"

"Morgan, I'm sure she's not involved. I mean, she's resentful of my position, but—"

Morgan looked up. "Resentful how?"

"I sense she's jealous that I connect so easily with the kids. She's more of a mother type and tends to lecture, so they shy away from her."

"Does she have children of her own?"

"She has a daughter. Her son died when he was a teenager. He got drunk and wrapped his car around a tree. Sometimes I feel like she's in this line of work to make up for not being there for him. It's so tragic, but it wasn't her fault."

Morgan wondered why she couldn't give herself that same kind of compassion and understanding in regards to Suzy.

"Has she ever made threats?"

"No, nothing like that."

"Where does she live, Jules?"

"Seattle. Ballard, I think."

"I'll check it out." Morgan walked her to his truck and opened the door. "Let's get you home."

Later that day, Julie and Edith had just started preparing supper when Lana called to check in, heard Mom was making her specialty—baked honey-nut chicken, broccoli and herbed biscuits—and invited herself over.

Mom had spent the day reorganizing, cleaning and washing windows to let in the light. The house almost felt warm and welcoming. Almost. The dark walls and cherry furniture still cast a bleak shadow throughout the downstairs living area. Julie knew that wouldn't last long if Mom had her way. Julie could just see Mom tying up her hair in her red bandanna and getting to work with a bucket of paint.

"Lana said Ashley might be joining her, and where Ashley goes, Sketch follows." Mom shot Julie a smile over her shoulder as she put the biscuits in the oven.

"Should we call Morgan and ask if that's okay?" Julie asked.

"He won't mind. He's very gracious that way, although he's been a bit cranky lately. Company will cheer him up."

"He's worried about his father, huh?" Julie rinsed broccoli spears in the sink.

"No, actually, I think he's made peace with the Lord about his father's condition. He's been more guarded since you came home."

"Why? I can't hurt him. He hates me."

"He could never hate you, sweetie."

"It's okay, I deserve it."

Mom turned off the water and with two gentle hands to her shoulders, turned Julie to face her. "Stop beating yourself up. We all make mistakes, and we're forgiven through the Lord's love."

"Do you think I made a mistake breaking up with Morgan?"

With a sigh, Mom rubbed her hand down Julie's arm. Just as she was about to speak, the back door burst open and Lana breezed into the kitchen, Ashley right behind her.

"Smells good," Lana said, cracking the oven door.

"Hey." Mom grabbed a dish towel and snapped it at Lana's backside. "No peeking. I just put those in."

"The chicken looks amazing, too." Lana smiled.

"What can I get you girls to drink?" Mom offered.

"I'm good," Lana said, flopping down at the kitchen table. "I overdid it on the cider."

"How about you, Ashley?"

"Do you have any hot chocolate?"

"I think Caroline dropped off cocoa in her care package yesterday. Let me see..."

As her mother dug into one of the two grocery bags, Julie sat next to Lana, and Ashley joined them.

"How was the rest of your day?" Julie asked.

"Fan-tastic. Most of the tourists came into the snack shop for lunch, which kept us busy."

"Do you make enough from tours and sandwiches to cover your expenses?"

"Yep, I always manage to break even. But I couldn't do it without this wonderful girl." Lana nodded at Ashley, who blushed. "How was *your* afternoon with Morgan?"

"Tense."

"I'll bet." Lana and Ashley snickered.

"We were going over case files for kids at Teen Life."

Lana cleared her throat. "Oh."

Julie hadn't meant to make her sister feel bad, but honestly, Lana had to stop teasing Julie about her non-romance with Morgan.

"Did you find anything?" Mom asked.

"Not yet. Ethan said my situation might not be related to my work."

"If not work, then what?" Lana said.

"That's the fifty-thousand-dollar question. Ethan suggested I might have upset someone."

"You?" Lana said with a hint of sarcasm.

"What?" Julie challenged.

"Oh, nothing." She smirked.

"No, I want to hear it." Julie leaned forward in her chair.

"Girls, no fighting."

"We're not fighting, we're discussing," Julie said.

"It's just…" Lana hesitated. "You can be pretty type A. I mean, if you think something should be done a certain way, you're not very open to other people's opinions."

"I listen to people."

Ashley's gaze bounced from Lana to Julie

and back again. She was probably thinking it hadn't been such a good idea to come for dinner.

"I'm not criticizing here," Lana said. "Lord knows I've got my share of challenges. But I can see where someone might take offense to your, let's call it, determined nature."

"You're saying I'm rigid?"

"I'm saying you are very clear about how things should go, which makes you a great leader."

"You mean bossy."

The back door swung open and Morgan stepped into the kitchen.

"Saved by the cops, praise the Lord," Lana greeted.

"What, something wrong?" Morgan suddenly looked worried.

"Sibling disagreement," Mom said.

"It's a good thing I have my sidearm," Morgan joked.

And just like that, the tension lifted. But Julie didn't forget her sister's comments, and although it stung, there was a ring of truth to them. Julie was determined and focused. To some that might come off as bossy, but was it enough of a motive to want to hurt her?

"What's for dinner?" Morgan asked.

"Honey-nut chicken, broccoli and biscuits,"

Mom said, sliding cocoa in front of Ashley. "I didn't think you'd mind a few extras for dinner."

"Not at all." Morgan walked over to the closet, took off his gun and put it in his lockbox.

A knock at the back door made Ashley jump up and open it. Sketch stood in the doorway, peering inside. "Hey."

"Hi," Ashley greeted.

Julie and Morgan exchanged a knowing glance.

"Invite him in," Lana encouraged.

"You sure it's okay, Mrs. Burns?" Sketch asked.

"I'd be offended if you didn't stay for dinner."

"In that case…" Sketch stepped into the kitchen and froze at the sight of Morgan. "Oh, I didn't know the chief was here."

"It's my dad's house, buddy. Where else would I be?"

"Work. You always seem to be working."

"I'm taking the night off."

"Completely off?" Sketch said.

"Completely. No danger of me grilling you about breaking into Rutger's computer and planting a monkey virus."

All eyes focused on Sketch. "What?" he defended. "Mr. Rutger overcharged Gram on the Impala."

"That's between your grandmother and Mr. Rutger, don't you think?" Morgan said.

"I thought you were off duty," Sketch countered.

Morgan put up his hands in surrender. "You're right. Sit down and have some cocoa. We'll talk monkey viruses tomorrow."

Sketch hesitated. Ashley slipped her hand into his and led him to the chair next to her. "It's okay," she said.

Her tone, the coaxing touch, reminded Julie of a time when she'd had to coax Morgan out of his shell, his dark place.

*You can't go back there. You can never go back.*

Julie turned to Morgan, who studied her with questions in his eyes.

"So, did you find anything on Helen?" Julie asked.

"Who's Helen?" Mom asked.

"A coworker."

"We'll discuss it later. If you're making cocoa, I could use a cup." Morgan sat beside Julie.

"Anyone else?" Mom asked. "I've got whipped cream and green and red Christmas sprinkles."

"Mom, let me help." Julie stood.

Mom waved her off. "I'm fine."

Morgan touched Julie's hand, warmth creeping up her arm. "Sit down, relax."

She glanced at Lana, expecting another smirk or wink. But she was deep into a discussion with Sketch about computer issues at Stone Soup.

Julie eased back into her chair, breaking contact with Morgan's hand. She loved the feel of his gentle touch, but didn't want to hurt him again. Keeping a physical and emotional distance was the best strategy.

"How did you spend your afternoon?" Morgan asked.

"Helping Mom, mostly. She's been sprucing up the place to get ready for Christmas."

"Speaking of which, where are your Christmas decorations, Morgan?" Mom asked.

"In a box somewhere," he said. His eyes dimmed and his jaw hardened.

"Can you be more specific? I'd love to decorate."

"Thanks, but it's not necessary."

Mom turned to Morgan. "Maybe not, but I'd love to do that for you and your dad, as a thank-you for letting us take up residence in his house."

"Really, there's no need."

Julie sensed something else was going on here, and didn't want Mom to keep pushing.

"What exciting things was the police chief

up to today other than trying to solve his ex-girlfriend's crisis?" Julie asked.

"Busywork. Boring to a city girl like you."

He was on the attack again. Probably defending himself from whatever he was hiding about the Christmas decorations.

"I'm still a small-town girl at heart," Julie heard herself say. And it was true.

The tension in his face eased. "Someone keyed Mrs. Meyers's car and someone else vandalized the public restroom in town."

"How do you know it was someone else?" Sketch said.

"You have something you want to share, kid?"

Sketch shifted back in his chair. "No, I... I just mean, I don't know, I just—"

Ashley must have squeezed his hand under the table, because he stopped talking.

"Hey, I'm not interrogating you," Morgan assured. "It just seems like vandalizing is a kid thing to do, and since you're a teenager you might have some insight into the subject."

"No, I don't have any insight." Sketch glanced down.

A hush fell over the room.

"Dinner's ready," Mom announced, followed by yet another knock at the door.

"Anderson probably smelled your cooking from next door and doesn't want to miss out."

Morgan went to answer the door and hesitated. He placed his hand on the teenager's shoulder and Sketch looked up at him.

"It's all good," Morgan said with a smile.

Morgan opened the door and a cop stood on the porch.

"Scott," Morgan greeted.

"Can I have a word outside?" the cop said. He looked to be in his twenties, with short, black hair and a serious expression.

"What's wrong?" Julie said.

"Nothing, ma'am. Sorry to interrupt. Police business."

Morgan joined him on the back porch and shut the door.

"Girls, help me set the table," Mom said.

Julie and Lana got up and pulled down plates and silverware, but Julie's attention was riveted on the men outside having a serious discussion. As if he sensed her watching him, Morgan glanced through the window and shot Julie a half smile.

She knew that smile. He was covering for something.

"Ashley, can you take over?" Julie asked.

"Sure."

Julie went onto the porch. "What is it?"

"Julie, this is Deputy Chief Scott Finnegan."

"Nice to meet you," Scott said.

"Something's happened, hasn't it?" she asked.

The deputy chief glanced at Morgan, but didn't answer.

"It can't be worse than what my imagination is dreaming up right now," Julie said. "Please, Morgan, tell me."

"A stranger in town." Morgan paused. "He's been asking about you."

# *Chapter Eight*

Morgan turned back to Scott, fearing if he looked too long at Julie's vulnerable expression, he'd lose it and pull her into his arms.

"City Hall and where else?" Morgan asked.

"The Turnstyle. Anna called me about it."

"Did she get a description?"

Scott referred to his notebook. "Fifties, fair-skinned, red hair. He was wearing jeans, a navy shirt, cargo-type jacket and black boots, like work boots. Plus, she got a partial plate number."

"That's pretty good for a civilian."

"What did you expect? She's been hanging out with the police chief."

Dead silence stretched between the three of them. Morgan felt as if he'd been caught doing something wrong. But he had no reason to feel that way. Whom he dated was his business.

"Anything else?" Morgan asked.

"She tried getting information out of him, but he was pretty guarded. Still, she found out he was from Seattle, has two kids and went to Seattle U. And—" Scott glanced at Morgan "—he asked for hotel suggestions."

"Did Anna recommend anything?"

"The Blue Goose and the Port Whisper Inn."

"Good girl," Morgan whispered.

"What? Why good girl?" Julie challenged.

"Because if he took her recommendations, we know where to find him."

"Do you think…?"

"I'm not thinking anything just yet." He turned back to Scott. "Did you run the plates?"

"Not yet."

"Do it."

"Yes, sir."

"What about fishing licenses for the island today?"

"Still working on it."

"Good, keep me posted."

Scott nodded at Julie. "Nice to meet you. Good night."

Morgan and Julie watched the deputy get into his cruiser and take off.

"How did they find me?" Julie said, with a trembling voice.

Morgan took her hands and gave them a gentle squeeze. "I'm not going to let anything happen to you, Jules. Let's go inside. I'll call the Blue Goose and Port Whisper Inn to see if anyone checked in today."

"The Port Whisper Inn," she said, wistful. "Morgan, I've put Caroline in danger."

"We don't know that. Honey—" he searched her eyes "—look at me."

She glanced up with teary golden eyes.

"None of this is your fault, okay?"

She nodded and he led her inside, where her mom was serving dinner to the chatty group.

"I don't get what would make the hard drive conk out like that," Lana said.

"Doesn't matter, as long as you have a backup," Sketch said.

"I have one—that doesn't mean I remember to use it."

"I can set you up with an auto-backup program so you don't have to think about it."

"Honey?" her mother asked. "Everything okay?"

Julie glanced at Morgan for guidance.

"We're not sure yet. Go ahead and eat. I need to make a few calls." Morgan slipped into the living room and pulled out his cell. He didn't want to alarm Sketch about the stranger staying at his grandmother's inn until Morgan knew what he was dealing with.

He called Caroline and she answered on the first ring.

"Port Whisper Inn."

"Caroline, it's Morgan Wright."

"Hi, Chief. What's wrong? Does Edith need something for the pie?"

"No, ma'am. I'm calling to find out if any strangers registered for a room today."

"No, we haven't had any new guests since Tuesday. Why?"

"Please give me a call if a male, fifties, wearing work boots and a cargo jacket, shows up to rent a room, okay?"

"Sure."

"Thanks."

He called the Blue Goose, but again, no one fitting the stranger's description had checked in. Morgan wasn't sure if he should be relieved or more concerned.

At least Anna had given it a good try. She was a smart girl, probably had guessed that Julie was in danger and figured if she gave the stranger hotel recommendations it would help Morgan locate him.

He called Anna to thank her. "Morgan, hi," she answered. "Is this about the guy who was asking about Julie?"

"Yes, I wanted to thank you for calling Scott and directing the man to the two properties."

"Did he check in?"

"Not yet, but I appreciate your effort."

"Anything for you, Morgan."

Morgan closed his eyes, not sure how to respond.

"Awkward..." Anna said. "Sorry, didn't mean to come on so strong."

"I should be the one apologizing."

"Why, because you've been dating me but you're in love with another woman?"

"Anna, I—"

"It's okay. I totally understand. If Dean were to walk back into my life after ten years, I'd drop you like a hot tamale. No offense."

"None taken."

"Just—" She hesitated. "Can we still grab dinner once in a while? You're a good listener."

"Dinner sounds great."

"Cool. You take care of yourself, and Julie."

"You're too good to me."

"Remember that the next time you pull me over for speeding."

"Will do."

"'Bye."

Ending the call, he turned to find Julie standing right behind him. He could tell by the look on her face that she'd overheard his sincere thanks, and had probably misinterpreted it.

Couldn't think about that now. He had to track down the stranger.

"He hasn't checked in to either the Blue Goose or the Port Whisper Inn," he said.

"He could be anywhere."

"We'll find him before he finds you."

She frantically paced the living room, wringing her hands. "I'm putting family and friends in danger." She stopped and stared him down. "I never should have come back."

She brushed past him and headed for the stairs.

"Where are you going?"

"To pack."

He grabbed her hand and she froze on the steps. "You know I can't let you go."

She snapped her head around and pinned him with teary golden eyes. "You have to. Just like before."

"This is not about—"

She leaned forward and kissed him.

Julie was losing her mind. Completely.

Heightened emotions ruled over all common sense and she acted on her most basic need: to connect with Morgan again. His warm lips melted the ball of fear in her chest. Then guilt smacked her upside the head.

She broke the kiss and glanced at the wooden floor. "I'm sorry, I'm so sorry."

Instead of scolding her, he took both her hands. "It's okay, sweetheart. I understand."

She glanced at him, waiting for him to expand on his comment. Instead, he shot her a humble half smile. "Let's go back inside."

"But the stranger—"

"Isn't going to find you here. My deputy chief will call if anything breaks. Just—" he brushed her cheek with his thumb "—take a deep breath and enjoy the moment."

"You mean…?" *The kiss?*

"Dinner with your family," he said.

He led her into the kitchen where Mom, Lana, Ashley and Sketch carried on a heated discussion.

"Everything okay?" her mother asked, glancing at Julie and Morgan.

"Fine, thank you. How's the chicken?" Morgan asked Sketch.

"Awesome."

Morgan let go of Julie's hand. She immediately missed its warmth.

"What's the topic of discussion?" Julie asked.

"Horizon Farms. It's a new community project they're opening outside of town," Lana said. "It's a place for troubled kids to straighten out their lives."

"The trouble is their parents," Sketch muttered.

"Why do you say that?" Mom pressed.

Julie eyed her chicken, wanting to enjoy the taste of Morgan's lips a minute longer.

"If kids are screwed up, it's because of their wacky parents."

"You mean kids don't have any responsibility for their actions? Even at seventeen and eighteen?" Morgan challenged.

"I'm saying, if the parents were normal the kids wouldn't have—" he made quotation marks with his fingers "—issues."

"I don't get that," Morgan said, cutting his chicken. "Teenagers want to be treated like adults, yet when things go wrong they blame their parents."

"You wouldn't understand. You had the perfect father," Lana said.

Julie kicked her sister under the table.

"What?" Lana protested.

"No one's perfect," Morgan said. "It's what you do with the situation you've been given that counts. Sketch decided to drop out of school and hack into computers."

"I haven't broken the law," Sketch defended. "Besides, school is dumb."

Morgan pinned him with a hard expression.

"You know what I think? I think you're a smart kid. You didn't fit in, so you acted out."

"Smart? I'm the high-school dropout, remember?"

"From what I've heard, you can do things with computers that would amaze engineers at Microsoft. So stop pretending you don't have the brains. It's insulting to those of us who struggled in school due to learning disabilities."

"You mean...you—"

"Yep." Morgan forked a piece of chicken. "I had two choices—feel sorry for myself, or plow on through. I chose the latter."

"Yeah, well, your dad was probably behind you all the way. My mom is too busy with Mackie to care about my life, and all the step-monster wants is for me to fail so he can ship me away somewhere."

"Sketch, that's not true," Mom said.

"What about your grandma?" Morgan shot back. "From what I've seen, she cares more than two sets of parents. You're lucky you've got her. I had a workaholic father and no mother. At some point I decided it didn't matter. I set my own goals, and met them."

As the discussion continued, Julie remarked on how much Morgan had changed. When they'd first started dating, he'd been insecure and angry, but over the years, he'd matured into a quality man with a personal strength that awed her. Sure, she'd brought him out of his shell in high school, but she couldn't take credit for the man seated next to her.

A man, she realized, who was not the same boy she'd left behind.

"What?" he said, eyeing her. He'd caught her smiling.

"Nothing." She buttered her biscuit and thought of the inappropriate kiss they'd just shared.

Inappropriate? Why? They were both adults, and he hadn't exactly pushed her away.

It was inappropriate because she didn't want to hurt him again, give him the wrong signals and set up an expectation she couldn't possibly meet.

No, although her impulse was a stupid one, it was just that: an impulse. She'd apologize later and explain that it was a kiss of gratitude. Morgan had a way of making her feel safe, even when she knew someone was close, stalking her. Heck, he could be down the street.

Just then, Morgan reached out and touched her arm. "Sound good?"

"I'm sorry, what?"

"We'll go to church services tomorrow at nine. Or is that too early for you?"

"Are you sure that's wise?" She didn't see the

value in sitting in a church where her stalker could easily figure out she might go on a Sunday morning.

"Well, we're not leaving you home alone," Mom said. "Everyone's going, right?"

"Of course," Lana said.

"Yes, ma'am," Ashley answered.

Everyone looked at Sketch. "Okay, okay. I'll be there."

"Got anything nicer than a T-shirt and jeans?" Morgan teased.

"Hey, I've been to church with Gram before."

"And we know she'll be there, because she's making the pastries for the reception after the service."

A reception. Great. Sitting in church for an hour would be hard enough, but socializing for another hour with the locals? Julie didn't have the energy for small talk, especially in her current edgy state.

The group broke into another round of discussion about Horizon Farms and the potential spike in crime in Port Whisper.

"We shouldn't assume that because these kids have had a rough journey that they're going to act out and cause trouble in town," Mom said. "What do you think, Chief?"

"I think—" he paused and glanced at Julie "—everyone deserves a second chance."

\* \* \*

The next day Julie found herself in church for the first time in six years. She remembered the week she'd stopped going, right after she'd lost her first client, Phillip Bratton, to a violent, gruesome death. And somehow after that, she'd had a hard time both coping with the pain and believing in God. Where was God when Phillip lay bleeding in the street?

The choir sang beautiful hymns, infused with love and celebration. She could almost feel the glory of God float across the congregation, who seemed enthralled by the music, the prayers and the sermon.

About forgiveness.

Julie fidgeted, dug in her purse and popped a cough drop. Anything to distract herself from Pastor Peterson's words. She just couldn't deal with them right now.

It wasn't just his words that made her anxious. It all felt so…foreign.

After the service, Morgan stayed close as Julie, Mom, Lana, Ashley and Sketch made their way to the community room where Caroline put out freshly baked scones, breads and Christmas cookies.

"Julie? Julie Burns?" A thirtysomething woman with a bright smile gave her a hug.

"Hey, yep, it's me."

The woman stepped back. "You don't remember me, do you? Wendy Metter, from biology?"

"Oh, right, Wendy. You look—wow, you look great."

Wendy had been height- and weight-challenged, and always had had a bubbly personality.

"Thanks. Married life agrees with me." Wendy motioned a tall man in a navy suit over. "Brian, this is a high-school friend, Julie Burns."

"Nice to meet you." He shook her hand.

"I can't believe you're here. And with Morgan." Wendy winked.

No matter how many times people did that, it still irked Julie.

"They were high-school sweethearts," Wendy explained to her husband. "Brian and I have been married just over a year. He came to town to help build the new resort, and never left."

"Tell me more about the resort," Julie asked, hoping to divert them from the topic of Julie and Morgan's non-romance.

Brian, a pleasant man, described the hundred-room resort, complete with indoor water park, live entertainment and spa. He seemed passionate about the project, and obviously adored Wendy. He would touch her sleeve and interlink his fingers with hers as he spoke. It made Julie happy to know such a sweet girl had found true love. She deserved it.

*And you don't?* a voice taunted.

"If you could excuse us," Morgan said to Wendy and Brian. "There's a peach-walnut scone over there with my name on it."

"Sure, sure." Wendy gave Julie another hug. "I'd love to catch lunch sometime."

"That sounds great."

"Are you at your mom's?" Wendy asked.

"No, actually we're staying at Morgan's dad's house."

The minute the words left her lips, she saw the wheels turning in Wendy's green eyes.

"Mom's having her floors redone and Morgan offered to let us stay there," Julie clarified.

"Oh, oh, right." But from Wendy's quirked eyebrow, she wasn't buying it.

"Nice meeting you," Julie said to Brian.

As Morgan led her away, Julie glanced over her shoulder and spotted Wendy whispering into her husband's ear.

"Jules," Morgan said, warning in his voice.

"What?"

"They don't mean any harm." He stepped up to the coffee urn and poured her a cup, complete with sugar and cream. "What did you think of the service?"

"Okay, I guess."

"Just okay, huh?"

"I'm sorry, Morgan. I'm not much into religion these days. I told you that."

"You don't have to be into religion to appreciate the sermon. Here, have a scone." With metal tongs, he put one on a plate and handed it to her.

Just then, the deputy chief, in full uniform, cut through the crowd, heading straight for Morgan. Julie's heart sped up. Had he discovered the identity of the stranger?

"Chief," Scott said. "Sorry to bother you at church."

"No problem, Scott."

Lana came up beside Julie. "Margaret Sloan's been asking about you. Come on."

Julie glanced at Morgan.

"Go ahead. I won't be far." Julie watched Morgan and Scott wander off into a quiet corner.

"Hey, don't worry. He's not going to leave you," Lana said.

Her sister's words hit Julie square in the chest. She realized how much she depended on Morgan, and not just for protection.

"Julie!" Margaret Sloan said, throwing her arms around Julie.

There'd been too much hugging today, too much socializing for Julie's taste.

"I hear you're in Seattle. As a social worker?"

"I counsel street kids and try to help them

find their way back to a healthy and stable life."
She sounded like an automaton. But it was safer
to click into professional mode than to expose
the intense emotions that tangled her stomach
into knots on most days when she worried about
the kids.

"Wow, I'm so not worthy," Margaret joked.
"I market party supplies. Hardly a worthwhile
endeavor compared to what you do."

"That's not true," Lana interjected. "If you
love your work, that's what counts. Look at me,
I run a tour business and sandwich shop. Hardly
glamorous, but I figure if I bring joy to one
person's life on any given day, I've done God's
work."

"How's the business going?" Margaret asked.

"It's seasonal," Lana said. "Although this year
I've increased December business by offering
Christmas packages and decorated the boat in
colorful lights for night cruises of the bay."

"If you ever need free marketing help, I'd be
happy to brainstorm."

"Awesome, thanks."

Julie half listened to the conversation while
spying across the reception hall to catch a
glimpse of Morgan. There was no sign of him.
She spotted his half-eaten scone and coffee cup
on the edge of a table.

Panic flooded her chest. Had the deputy chief

found the stranger? What if Morgan went with Scott to check out the stranger's motel room and the man had a gun?

"Excuse me for a second," she said to Lana and Margaret.

She made a beeline for the front door of the church, hoping that Morgan and Scott were just outside. She flung open the door, but they were nowhere in sight.

Walking toward the parking lot, someone called out her name.

"Julie Burns?"

She turned and spotted a man in his fifties with red hair and pale skin.

"Yes?" Her gaze drifted down…to his black work boots.

She took a step back, chiding herself for leaving a church full of people to come outside where she stood alone with the stranger.

"I've been looking for you."

# Chapter Nine

Instincts on red alert, Julie took off toward the front of the church, hoping to find safety inside.

"Miss Burns!" he called after her.

She whipped open the front door to the church, and Morgan gripped her upper arms.

"Hey, what's wrong?"

"That guy…who was looking for me with the boots—"

"It's okay. He's not an enemy." Morgan pulled her to his chest and stroked her back. "A misunderstanding. We checked him out. He's one of the good guys."

She tipped her head back. "What do you mean?"

"I'm sorry for scaring her, Chief." The man came up behind them.

"Julie, this is Joe Wilson of Horizon Farms," Morgan said by way of an introduction.

She turned around and eyed the man, hesitated. "I don't understand."

"I can explain over lunch, if you'll let me. The chief's invited, as well." Joe extended his hand, and she shook it.

"I don't think I can wait until lunch," Julie said. She wanted answers sooner rather than later.

"I don't want to keep you from your friends inside."

"I really need an explanation." Julie wasn't anxious to go back in anyway.

"Well, I'd like to take my time explaining it to you, but I understand your curiosity. I'm managing director of Horizon Farms. Have you heard of it?"

"The facility for teenagers trying to get their lives back on track?"

"'Facility' sounds a bit clinical. It's a farm where kids will build their own housing, care for the animals and grow vegetables. The visionary, Elizabeth Quinn, lost a son to drug abuse, and came up with the concept to give kids like her son an alternative path to heal. She had a theory that hardworking teenagers are productive and healthy teenagers."

"Had?"

"She passed away six months ago. Named me her executor and manager of Horizon. It took us this long to locate property we thought suitable for the project."

"I'm confused. What does this have to do with me?"

"I've done research on the area and the people of Port Whisper. Many times causes like this can create fear and anxiety in a community, yet we need support from the locals to make it work. Anyway, your name came up repeatedly as a success story, a woman who's dedicated her life to working with teenagers. You both know the community and understand the need to help kids get on track. I could use your advice on how to ingratiate myself into the community."

"I haven't lived here in a very long time," Julie said.

"Yes, but home is home. These folks respect and trust you."

"What are you asking me to do, exactly?"

"Listen to my proposal, give me feedback on our plan. It's a good one, modeled after a very successful program in Utah. Most of all, if you see its value, and only if you see the value, I'd appreciate your support in our venture. However, if you don't, I would understand."

Julie couldn't quite wrap her head around it: the stranger-stalker was not a threat. He was a man trying to help teenagers.

Just like her.

"It's a lot to process, I know. That's why I was hoping to take you to lunch. Not today, of course. I know you have family obligations." Joe motioned toward the church.

"Would you like to join us?" Morgan asked.

"I know how people talk about strangers. I want to ease into things before they find out I'm with Horizon."

"You're right, people do talk. Which is why you should come in and let me introduce you around," Morgan said. "People are most frightened of what they don't understand. I think once they meet you, they'll warm up quick enough."

"I agree," Julie added. "If they're comfortable around you, they'll open up, and will feel like they can share their concerns. Truthful and open communications should be your primary goal."

"Of course."

Morgan motioned Joe inside. "Grab some coffee. Jules and I will join you in a minute."

The church door closed behind him, and Morgan tipped her chin up to look into his eyes. "You okay?"

"Better now, yeah." And she was, whenever she looked into Morgan's eyes.

"I'm sorry I didn't get to you before you saw Joe. Scott did a background check and Joe is who he says he is, a former businessman looking to transition into more fulfilling, altruistic work. He's married with two grown children, and he's looking for a place to stay. I think I've talked him into renting a room at the Port Whisper Inn."

"Where's his wife?"

"She'll stay in the city until Horizon is up and running. Probably won't be until next spring or summer. There's a lot of work to be done, including getting permits from the city."

"It sounds like a wonderful program. How do you think it will be received?"

"That kind of depends on us, and other leaders in Port Whisper. He's right, Julie. People trust you, and they trust me. I'd like to hear a little more about the program so we can form an educated opinion."

Morgan opened the door for her. "I gotta say, it's nice to have the distraction."


Julie met with Joe Wilson the next day and they discussed Horizon Farms and the organization's goal of helping kids. It was a worthy cause, for sure, but would the residents of Port Whisper embrace the idea?

Morgan was right. People tended to be afraid of things they didn't understand, things that seemed threatening. But she also knew that with the proper support, lost teenagers could get a second chance.

"It's an admirable endeavor," Julie said, sitting across from Joe at the Turnstyle restaurant. Morgan sat next to her.

"I'm glad you think so," Joe said. "The real challenge is making the community feel a sense of ownership in the program."

"Tell me about your prospective residents." She sipped her coffee.

"We're trying to get to kids before they self-destruct and take to the streets. We'll promote this program to parents of kids who are failing in school. I believe failing is an indicator that a kid has given up."

"Will they live on the property?"

"Yes. They will build the dorms with their own hands. They'll take shifts planning out meals for the week and maintaining the grounds. We'll encourage them to get jobs in Port Whisper or Port Angeles, grades and time permitting. Since it's an hour to Port Angeles and half an hour to Port Whisper, we'll provide transportation."

"Where will they attend school?"

"We'll run our own program with certified teachers."

"Have any kids signed up yet?"

"A dozen boys. Ten more have applied. We have a comprehensive interview process. They're good kids. Just lost."

"You should have a town meeting to introduce them. Show people that there's nothing to be afraid of."

"Good idea." He jotted in his notebook. "My wife and I will move into the main house next month, then if all goes well, construction will begin in May, providing the weather cooperates. We hope to launch the program this summer."

Morgan shifted in the booth. "Sorry to interrupt, but we need to get going."

She sat up straight. "What's wrong?"

"Nothing. I've got some things to check on at work and need to drop you at home."

"Thanks for meeting with me," Joe said, shaking her hand.

"My pleasure. Here's my cell number if you want to chat some more."

Morgan escorted her to his truck and they headed for his dad's house.

"Are you sure everything's okay?" she asked.

"Fine, just work stuff."

"Related to my case?"

"Sort of, but nothing serious," he said.

"Meaning what?"

"The mayor's breathing down my neck."

"Why?"

"He's critical of the way I've handled things."

"In what way?"

"He's worried that you've brought trouble to

Port Whisper and it could put residents in danger."

"He's right," she said.

He leveled her with a stern look. "I'm the police chief and it's my job to protect the citizens, which includes you, Jules."

"Could this jeopardize your job?"

"No, but it's hard to take criticism from someone who knows little about law enforcement. It'll be fine. Promise."

They pulled into the driveway and Morgan walked her up to the house. "Stay put. I'll be home for dinner."

He hesitated, as if he were a husband about to kiss his wife's cheek before saying goodbye.

She saw an opening and went for it. She had to clarify last night's kiss. "Listen, about the kiss—"

"We don't have to talk about it."

"But we do. It was a thank-you kiss, Morgan. You always know how to calm me down and make me feel like everything's going to be okay. It was an automatic response of gratitude."

"Okay, right." He broke eye contact and glanced into the house. "You'd better get inside. I'll see you later."

He turned and climbed down the stairs. She watched him pull out of the drive, still not making eye contact. Guilt tangled her insides. It was the right thing to do. She had to set the record straight so he didn't develop inappropriate feelings for her.

Much like she had in the past few days. It was to be expected considering the dangerous situation: Julie on the run and Morgan acting as protector. Inappropriate or not, they felt genuine and intense, and somehow she'd have to put them in a box and lock them up.

The front door swung open and Mom greeted her. "I thought I heard someone on the porch. Where's Morgan?"

Julie and her mother went into the house. "Had to go to work. He said he'd be back for dinner."

"Good, we should be done with the first coat of paint by then."

"Hi, Julie," Caroline greeted, as she rolled a coat of paint on the dark wall.

"Can I help?" Julie offered.

"No, you relax. Read a good book or take a nap," Mom said.

Julie wasn't one for sitting around. "I'm pretty good at painting."

"We've got it," Caroline said. "There's cookies in the kitchen."

"Thanks, but if I keep eating like this I'll gain ten pounds."

Julie took off her coat, grabbed a book off a

pile on the coffee table and flopped down on the sofa.

She spent the rest of the afternoon lounging and reading, something she rarely did back in Seattle. Julie offered again to help with the painting project, but realized Mom enjoyed watching Julie take it easy. She knew how work consumed Julie's life, and probably felt as if she was being a good mother by forcing her to relax.

It was a foreign feeling for Julie, but for a few hours she lost herself in a cozy mystery about a ladies' tea group that fancied themselves detectives. Peppered with humor and emotion key to girlfriends' relationships, the book allowed Julie to escape into another world where the clues were set out in front of you, and everything would wrap up nicely by the end.

Between reading about the girlfriends in the book and watching Mom and Caroline dive into the painting project, it struck Julie how isolated she'd been since college. She had no close girlfriends to go to dinner with, or take in a movie.

"Good thing Angela Kotter could find alternate day care for the twins," Caroline said. "Can you imagine the mess they'd make if they were here today?"

Mom shuddered. "I'd rather not. I have to figure out what to get them for Christmas. They really are good kids, even if they have a precocious streak."

Caroline proceeded to tell a story about her grandson Mack who was quite the character, and Mom laughed and offered advice. The tone of the conversation changed when Sketch's name came up. Worry colored Caroline's voice.

"Hey, Caroline?" Julie closed her book.

"Yes, sweetie?"

"Sketch is a good kid. I don't think you have to worry about him."

"Thanks, but it comes with the job. Worry about your kids, worry about your grandkids, worry about your friends' kids, et cetera, et cetera."

"Has Sketch's behavior changed in the past six months?" Julie asked.

"No, it's been pretty consistent since he moved in with me."

"Where are his parents?"

"Spokane. I watched the kids while they were away. When Olivia and her husband came to get them, well, Sketch didn't want to leave. I think it was a combination of not getting along with his stepfather and Sketch's romance with Ashley. We decided Sketch would be better off staying with me, helping with the inn, that sort of thing."

"How did Sketch feel about that?" Julie asked.

Caroline dipped the roller in the paint. "He acted like it's what he wanted, but I suspect he feels abandoned. I'm just glad Ashley is in his life."

"Ah, high-school romance." Julie sighed.

The women shared a knowing glance. Julie redirected the conversation. "I've got some suggestions for Sketch if you're open to hearing them."

"Suggest away."

Mom shot Julie a proud smile.

"Convince him to study for his GED and find him a mentor. I suspect he's very bright and would pass the GED on the first try. You only need to score fifty percent to pass."

"I didn't know that."

"And what about a job outside of the inn?"

Caroline sighed. "He's got a reputation in town ever since he put a monkey virus on my mechanic's computer."

"Why not use his brilliant computer skills to help people? He's been helping Lana with her business computer. She'd be a reference. Sketch could print up cards and go to Chamber of Commerce meetings to network. A few choice clients would really boost his self-esteem. You build that up and he'll get to the point where he wants to go to school to become a software engineer."

Caroline put down her roller, walked across

the room and gave Julie a hug. "Thank you, thank you so much for seeing the goodness in Steven."

"They've all got goodness, we just have to look a little harder with some."

Caroline went back to rolling cream-colored paint on the wall and Julie smiled to herself. It felt good to offer insight and advice, to focus on the possibilities for Sketch instead of the dire circumstances of a boy destined for tragedy.

The back door slammed shut announcing Morgan's arrival. She sat up, excited to see him.

*Watch it, girl.*

"I like the mentor idea," Mom offered, rolling paint.

"Yes, but who would be brave enough to take on a kid with his attitude?" Caroline said.

On cue Morgan wandered into the living room.

"Morgan is perfect," Julie said.

"Excuse me?" Morgan raised an eyebrow.

Julie blushed. "We were talking about finding Sketch a mentor."

"Ah, right. And I fit the job description because…?"

"You're someone to be admired, Chief," Mom chimed in. "You're a reliable, quality human being."

"Thanks, I think." Morgan eyed the living

room, already brightened by the first coat of paint. "You ladies do good work. I should be paying you by the hour."

"You just keep my daughter safe. That's payment enough," Mom said.

"I plan to." He sat on the couch next to Julie.

"Any word from Ethan?" Julie asked.

"Nothing today. He's probably got the day off."

Unfortunately, as they both knew, her stalker didn't take days off.

Morgan reached over and touched her hand. "I'm sure he'll call the minute he has any news."

For half a second, as she gazed into his colorful eyes, she wondered how she could have left this man. Their connection was so powerful, so pure.

Her cell vibrated, shocking her out of the tender moment.

She slipped it out of her pocket. "Hello?"

"Julie, it's Helen from work."

"Helen? How did you get this—?"

"William is in the hospital, thanks to you."

# Chapter Ten

Julie clenched the phone. "What?"

"He was attacked by people looking for you. What have you gotten yourself into, and how could you put the rest of us in danger like this?"

"I didn't—"

"Save it. Here, he wants to talk to you."

"Jules? What is it?" Morgan said. But she couldn't focus on anything but William.

"Julie?" William said in a raspy voice.

She stood, pacing across the living room with nervous energy. "What happened?"

"I was leaving work last night and two guys grabbed me. They wanted to know where you were but I told them I didn't know." He coughed and the line went quiet for a second.

"William?" She clutched the phone.

"He can't talk right now," Helen said. "But he wanted to let you know he was okay, which he most certainly is not. What kind of trouble did you get into?"

"I don't know exactly. I didn't mean—"

"Grow up and take some responsibility for yourself. Your cute blond highlights and effusive smile can't get you out of this one. I don't really care what you're into, just stop involving the rest of us, you self-absorbed, arrogant princess."

"Helen, don't," William said in the background.

"No, it's about time someone told her how we—"

"Julie, ignore her," William said into the phone. "She's worried about me."

"What's your condition?"

"Broken ribs, concussion, sprained arm. Nothing serious."

"You were attacked because of me! William, I am so sorry."

"It's okay, truly. Stop it, Helen."

"I want to talk to her," she said in the background.

Julie wasn't sure how much more scolding she could take. She was beating herself up enough for the both of them.

"Can you behave?" he said to Helen. "Okay, Julie, I'm going to pass the phone to Helen. Don't worry about me. I'll be fine, but I wanted to let you know about the attack. I didn't tell them anything other than you were staying with an old friend. I hope I didn't blow it."

"No, you did great. Take care of yourself."

"You, too."

A second later Helen came back on. "Don't let him fool you. It's worse than he's letting on."

"How much worse?"

"We don't know. We're waiting for results from an MRI."

"Keep me posted?"

The line went dead and Julie stared at her phone.

"Jules?" Morgan stroked her back.

Mom and Caroline had put down their rollers and closed ranks.

Julie looked at each of them, fighting back tears, tears of regret for putting her friend in danger.

"Someone attacked my friend William. They were looking for my location. He's in the hospital."

"But he's okay?" Morgan asked.

"I'm not sure. He says so, but Helen claims it's more serious than he's letting on."

"Helen?" Morgan said.

"She's the one who called, she…" She took a deep breath. "She let me have it for getting William involved in this mess."

Morgan framed her cheeks with gentle hands and looked deep into her eyes. "You did no such thing. I will not permit you to blame yourself for what happened."

"He's right, honey," Mom said, putting her arm around Julie. "This isn't your fault."

Anger rushed up her chest. She stepped away from Morgan and Mom and paced the living room. "If it weren't for me, William wouldn't have been attacked." She spun around to face them. "What if they track me down? Hurt one of you, or Lana? Argh!" She fisted her hands and anxiously tapped them against her hips.

"We're taking every precaution to prevent them from hurting you or anyone else in your family," Morgan said.

"How about informing the Community Cares group about the situation?" Caroline said.

Julie stopped pacing and eyed her. "Then everyone will know how badly I messed up."

"It will help us close ranks to protect you," Mom said. "It's like Neighborhood Watch on overdrive. It worked great last year when Arthur suffered from a head injury. He'd get confused and wander around. Nearly everyone in town knew about his condition and we all pitched in to protect him."

"That's not a bad idea," Morgan said.

"I've got a better one." Julie planted her hands to her hips. "I disappear."

"Oh, honey," Mom said. "We've talked about this. Running never solves anything. Your problems follow you until you face them head-on."

"And I will, but not here, where I'm putting all of you in danger."

"Knock it off," Morgan said.

The room went quiet.

"I'm tired of you feeling sorry for yourself, getting scared and running away," he said. "I'm not letting you get away with it this time. You're going to stay in Port Whisper and let us protect you. Got it?"

Morgan had had enough. He snapped, right there in front of Jules, Edith and Caroline.

For a brief second he worried that he sounded too much like his father: domineering and overbearing, bordering on violent.

"He's right," Edith added. She didn't look shocked or frightened by his outburst. She looked appreciative.

"I can call Anderson and ask him to call an emergency meeting of Community Cares," Caroline offered.

"Sounds good," Morgan said, not taking his eyes off Julie.

She had that panicked look, the kind an animal has right before sprinting away from danger.

"I'll speak with the mayor and village trustees to let them know what's going on," Morgan said.

"Do I get a say in this?" Julie crossed her arms over her chest.

"If you're speaking from your intellect, not your emotions," he said. Perhaps it was too harsh, but it was the truth. Leading with emotions meant disaster on so many levels. Especially where Morgan and Julie were concerned.

"I appreciate what you're all trying to do," Julie said.

"But?" Morgan pressed.

"The first thing I have to do is visit William in the hospital."

"That's not your intellect talking," Morgan said. "It's not safe."

"We went to Seattle to check out my apartment and visit your dad," she protested.

"No one knew we were coming," Morgan said. "This time there's a reason for you to return, and if these guys are smart they'll be staking out the hospital."

"It's heartless not to go," Julie protested. "He's my friend, and he needs me."

"You need to stay safe." He admired her loyalty, but leaving Port Whisper was not wise.

Edith accompanied Caroline into the kitchen to make the call. Julie continued her frustrated pacing of the living room. She wandered to the front window and turned to him, a hardened look in her eye.

"I can't do this anymore," she said.

"What?"

"Be terrified all the time, and guilty. It's draining."

Morgan took her hands. "In these situations, when everything looks lost and I don't know what to do… I pray."

She opened her mouth to protest, but he placed his forefinger on her lips. "Just humor me. I'm going to say a prayer and all I ask is that you take a moment to ground yourself with the feel of my hands holding yours, okay?"

She shrugged.

He closed his eyes and bowed his head. "Dear Lord, we pray for strength to see us through the challenging days ahead, and we pray for guidance to help us make the best decisions to keep Julie safe. Praise be to God, Amen."

He opened his eyes and was surprised that Julie's face was still bowed. He waited a second, giving her time, hoping she'd found solace in the moment.

She sighed and opened her eyes, but didn't let go of his hands. He searched her eyes.

She shot him a half smile. "Okay, that wasn't so bad."

He gave her hands a squeeze and let go. "I'm glad. Now, let's strategize security measures. What did William tell his attackers?"

"That I'd moved in with an old friend."

"That's vague enough."

"But if they figure out I grew up in Port Whisper—"

"Let go of the fear, Jules. It's the enemy of both intellect and emotion."

"Wow, don't you sound mature," she teased.

"I'm taking off, kids," Caroline said, walking into the living room. "Thanks again for your advice about Sketch, Julie. And thanks, Morgan, for offering to mentor Sketch."

"I did? When?" He shot her that charming smile.

"Your mom's making spaghetti and meatballs for dinner. Enjoy." She hugged Julie and left out the front door.

"Meatballs," Morgan said. "I'm never going to let you guys leave."

For a second he wondered if his comment made Julie uncomfortable.

She smiled and said, "I know what you mean. I'm going to miss Mom's home-cooked meals. I should probably offer to help."

"Good idea. I'll get changed." He headed for

the stairs, strategizing more ways to tighten security around Julie and her family without making them feel like prisoners.

"Morgan?"

He glanced at her.

"Thanks again, for everything."

"I told you, no thanks necessary. It's my—"

"—job, I know. It's been a long time since I could depend on someone like this." With a cute shrug, she turned and went into the kitchen.

He was going to say it was his pleasure to protect her, not his job. It was probably a good thing she'd interrupted him. He sensed she was still guarded when it came to their relationship, both past and present.

Climbing the stairs to the second-floor office, he realized the possibility of a present-day relationship with Jules had worked its way from dream to reality. But could he leave his post as police chief and follow her into the city?

He shut the office door and stared into the mirror above the dresser. "You're nuts," he said. He had no reason to think she was opening her heart to him again.

No reason except for that amazing kiss. Gripping the wooden dresser, he remembered the feel of her soft lips; their sweet taste had haunted him all night. It was a kiss of thanks, mixed with desperation. Suddenly the taste grew bitter in his mouth. He didn't want her kissing him out of gratitude or fear.

Did he want her kissing him at all? Wasn't that just another open door to disaster? Undoubtedly. He wasn't a foolish man, but Anna had pegged it: although he'd dated Anna, his heart still belonged to another woman.

Morgan and Julie's connection hadn't died completely, and he knew after a few more days, she'd feel it, too, if she hadn't already.

"Stay focused on the case," he scolded, unbuttoning his uniform shirt. He'd just given her the lecture on emotions clogging a person's judgment. He'd better take his own advice and shelve these runaway thoughts until they found the perps who were after her.

Then, after everything died down, perhaps he'd test the waters and get a sense of whether there was a future for them. If he spotted red flags along the way, he'd let it go once and for all.

But he needed to try one more time, or he'd always wonder.

A few days passed with no word from Ethan. Julie used the lull to cajole Morgan to take her to see William in Seattle, but he wasn't giving in. When Julie called, William had been discharged from the hospital, so his injuries weren't as serious as Helen let on.

She wasn't leaving Port Whisper until this case was resolved and he knew she'd be safe. There was no arguing with him.

By Wednesday, she was losing her mind. She'd read all the cozy mysteries Caroline had brought over and refused to watch daytime television. Mom still wouldn't let Julie help with the remodeling or meal prep.

Julie was an active person by nature, always running from one place to another, checking on kids, collecting and bringing them supplies. All this sitting around with nothing to do only fueled her anxiety over what was happening with the stalker, with Andy and Dane. She had to shift her energy toward something productive.

Morgan stopped by at lunchtime. As he leaned against the counter drinking a hot cup of cocoa, Julie broached the subject.

"I need a change of scenery," she announced.

"We'll take a drive," he offered.

"I don't want to get you in more trouble with your boss. Lana could use help at work."

"Not a good idea."

"Morgan, I feel like a caged animal."

"It'll be over soon."

"We don't know that."

"You can't—"

"I have to. Sitting here doing nothing only reminds me how much this crazy person is ruling my life. I decided not to be afraid anymore and not to let him control me. There has to be a way to find a balance here, Morgan."

He sighed and placed his cup on the counter. "Lana's business is too isolated. When she's not giving tours, it's just her and Ashley in the office. What if I got you a temporary job helping out at the Turnstyle?"

"As a server? Perfect."

"A dishwasher." He winked. "I don't want you exposed too much. At least you'll feel like you're contributing, and they could certainly use the help. Jimmy Jakes recently came down with mono and he's out for three weeks. If you promise to stay in back, out of sight..."

"I do." She put up a three-fingered Scout's Honor salute. As long as she got out around people, she could take her mind off her utter helplessness.

"Okay, let me give Lew a call. He'll have to run it by his staff."

Meaning Anna. Would she discourage Lew from bringing Julie on because of Anna's feelings for Morgan?

"Will it make Anna uncomfortable if I'm there?" she asked.

"Why would it?" He pulled out his cell and dialed.

"Because you and she…"

He glanced at her. "We're friends, nothing more."

"Are you sure?"

"Hey, Lew? It's Chief Wright. Listen, I have a favor. My friend Julie… Yes, that's her. She's looking for work and I thought… Right. Immediately?" He eyed Julie.

She nodded enthusiastically.

"Good, how about an hour?" Morgan said. "And that shift ends? Great, I'll pick her up at four. Thanks."

He pocketed his phone. "You're all set. But the ground rules are no floating around the restaurant—"

"When have I ever floated?"

"You stay in back and listen to your instincts. If the hairs rise on the back of your neck, trouble's close. You call me, got it?"

"Promise."

"You'd better eat something before we go. They get pretty busy and I doubt you'll have time for a break."

Morgan wasn't kidding. Three hours and a gazillion dishes later Julie was barely keeping up and hadn't had time for a breather. Helping out a local business was hard, but good work, and it distracted her from thinking about her stalker.

"We're running short on coffee mugs," Anna said, breezing into the kitchen.

"Okay, I, uh…" Julie reached for a handful of mugs, and knocked over a pitcher, sending it crashing to the floor. "Rats. I'll pay for it."

"Hey, relax, it's not a crisis," Anna said.

But it felt like one. Julie couldn't keep up and she hated feeling like a failure, much like she felt when she lost another boy to drug abuse.

She bent down to scoop up the big pieces and Anna got the broom.

"Go ahead and wash some mugs," Anna said. "I'll clean up."

"Thanks." Julie went back to the dishes.

"We really appreciate you coming in today," Anna said, sweeping shards of glass into the dustpan. "We couldn't have done it without you."

"Yeah, give me enough time and I'll break all your dishes," she joked.

Anna finished sweeping up the mess and hesitated. "Listen, I'm sorry about what's happening to you. If there's anything I can do…"

"Just letting me work here has been a great distraction. Although—" she took a breath

"—I'm sorry if my presence here has interfered with…well, with you and Morgan."

"We're just good friends."

Yet Julie sensed the first time she met Anna that the woman had hoped for more.

"That's too bad. You seem like you'd make a great couple," Julie offered, and she meant it. Anna was smart and cute, with a bubbly personality.

"I won't lie," Anna said, refilling a jam holder. "At one point I thought it could be more."

"But…?"

"His heart is spoken for." She winked.

Julie shook her head. "That was a long time ago."

"What are you afraid of?" Anna pressed.

"Excuse me?"

"It's obvious how you two feel about each other. Some people go through life and never find that kind of love. You guys had it once, and I still see it in both your and Morgan's eyes."

"You don't know me that well," Julie said, sounding rude, which wasn't her intent, but she got edgy whenever someone broached the subject of her and Morgan being in love again.

"True, but you're not that hard to read," Anna said. "I just hope when your situation is resolved, that you'll give him a chance. This whole star-crossed lovers thing is too painful to watch."

Anna went to the order counter, slid plates onto a tray and carried it into the restaurant.

Her words echoed in Julie's mind. Was that what she and Morgan were? Star-crossed lovers?

The back door opened and Morgan stepped into the kitchen. Instead of greeting Julie, he went to speak with the owner and cook, Lew Potter.

"You need to keep this door locked, Lew."

"Sorry, Chief. But then you wouldn't be able to wander in and flirt with your girlfriend," he joked.

Morgan sighed and shook his head as if surrendering to the town gossip. "Just keep it locked, okay?"

"No problem."

Morgan wandered over to Julie, who furiously washed mugs, rinsed them, dipped them in the sanitizing sink and put them on the drying rack.

"They keeping you busy?" he said.

"Yep." She couldn't look at him, not yet. The whole star-crossed lovers comment was still swirling in her brain.

"What's wrong?" he said.

"Multitasking was never my strong suit. Runs in the family."

"You have plenty of others."

"Gee, thanks, Chief." She winked, trying to lighten the moment. It was getting harder to keep any distance between them. Old habits were easy to fall into, like old shoes. They always felt comfortable. Even if they were worn out.

"You ready to go?" Morgan said.

"My shift isn't over until four." She leaned over to eye the clock. "I've got another hour."

"I thought you might have had enough."

"Oh, you think I'm that kind of employee, do you?" She realized this was the first time since they'd reunited that she didn't feel awkward or scrutinized. Thanks to dual focus on the dishes and the conversation, she couldn't overanalyze every word spoken, or every look they shared.

She glanced up and caught him eyeing her.

"What?" she said.

"Nothing. They scheduled a Community Cares meeting at Evergreen Church tonight at seven."

"Sounds good."

"I'll be back in an hour. I'll knock four times on the back door. Lew?"

"Yeah, Chief?"

"Four knocks is me. No one else gets back here as long as Julie's working for you."

"Got it."

Morgan headed to the door but stopped. "Hey, Julie?"

"Yeah?" She glanced up.

"I don't want to upset you by saying this, but it is really good to have you back." He shrugged. "Even if it's just temporary."

The door closed behind him and she stared at it for a second. Oddly enough, he didn't upset her with his words. As she redirected her attention to the dishes, she thought about the past week, being cared for by her mom and Caroline, watched over by Morgan and generally welcomed back by community friends.

Small towns offered something that cities never could: connection. City life felt so anonymous and detached at times. Julie didn't mind since her job was her main focus. But now, seeing how everyone helped each other out—Community Cares calling a meeting, and Lew letting her work in his kitchen—melancholy washed over her.

"Yikes!" Anna cried, as she skidded on the floor. A tray of dishes went flying.

Julie rushed over to her. "You okay?"

"Nothing broken but my ego. And here you thought you were a klutz."

Julie grabbed a bus tub and picked up broken pieces of plates.

"Hey, I'm not going to make you clean up my mess," Anna said.

"Looks like you spilled coffee on your uniform." Julie motioned to a stain on Anna's shirt. "You got another one?"

"Yeah, and a pair of spare jeans." She stood.

"Go on, I got this."

"If Henry Fritz comes looking for his pie, tell him to hold his horses."

"Will do."

Anna stood up and brushed herself off. "That's why I was in a hurry, because I kept forgetting his cherry pie. I don't know what's wrong with me today."

Julie stacked unbroken plates and mugs in the tub.

"Be back in a jiff." Anna ducked into the bathroom.

As Julie wiped up spilled coffee, a tall, elderly gentleman approached. "Miss? I saw Anna slip. Is she okay?"

"She's fine. She'll be right out. Are you Mr. Fritz?"

"Yes."

"I'll get your pie out to you in a sec, okay?"

"Thank you." He turned and went back to his table.

Julie finished cleaning up and asked Lew for a slice of cherry pie à la mode with extra whipped cream. She delivered it to Mr. Fritz and as she rushed back to the kitchen, another customer snagged her and asked for fresh coffee, then a third stopped her to ask about his French fries. As she jotted down the table number and "fries," a customer's voice drifted to her from the counter.

A familiar voice.

"Not yet, but I'm close. I'll find her and finish this in a day or two."

She glanced up.

At the back of the man from the ferry.

# Chapter Eleven

*I'll find her and finish this in a day or two.*

He was talking about Julie. He had to be. What were the chances that the very man who'd followed her on the ferry to give her her change had just happened to visit Port Whisper?

Snapping her gaze from the man, she forced a smile on her face as she passed a young family crowding a booth. *Act calm, pleasant, normal,* she reminded herself.

She wasn't going to let fear paralyze her. The man couldn't do anything in a crowded restaurant, and besides, he hadn't even seen her.

As she turned the corner to the kitchen, she bumped into Anna.

"Hey, you're not supposed to be out there."

"The booth up front needs coffee, the table with the lumberjack guy needs fries and I need to make a call."

"You okay?"

"Sure, sure." She waved her off and went into the storage closet for privacy. She pressed one on her phone and waited.

"Chief Wright."

"It's Julie. The guy from the ferry, he's sitting at the counter."

"Where are you right now?"

"In the storage closet."

"Did he see you?"

"No, I don't think so."

"And you're sure it's him?"

"Yes. I overheard his phone conversation. He said he'd find her and he'd finish it in a day or two. I think he was talking about me." Her pulse quickened as she repeated the words. Was he the man hired to find and perhaps kill her?

"How many people are in the restaurant?"

"It's nearly full. Morgan, you don't think—"

The door whipped open and Morgan reached out his hand, ending the call. "I'm calling Deputy Chief Finnegan to take you to Dad's. In the meantime, stay back here. You can come out of the closet, but don't leave this kitchen, got it?"

"Yes."

"It's going to be okay." He brushed her cheek with his thumb.

It was a gentle touch, a calming touch. With a nod, he walked away. He glanced around the corner, shot Julie a comforting smile and disappeared into the dining room.

Placing her hand to her cheek where his thumb had warmed her skin, she sensed it was a goodbye touch. The threat was sitting not fifty feet away. Once Morgan took the man in for questioning, they would all have answers to who was stalking Julie and why. The ferry man would lead them to the source of this nightmare, they'd hopefully find Dane and this would be over.

Julie would get her life back.

A life without Morgan.

She paced the kitchen, careful not to expose herself to the customers out front. Anxiety skittered across her nerve endings. Would Ferry Man make a scene? Fight Morgan? Did Morgan at least wait for backup?

*Heck, girl, this is a small town. There isn't any backup.*

She paced, fisted her hand. She stared at the clock, watching the second hand tick away.

Anna came into the back with an order ticket in hand.

"What's happening out there?" Julie asked Anna.

"You mean Morgan?"

Julie nodded.

"I just saw him and Scott escort a guy to Morgan's Jeep, why? Is he a bad guy from Seattle?"

"Yes—no—I don't know for sure. He didn't give Morgan any trouble?"

"Nope. Very polite guy. Left me a twenty-two-percent tip."

"Great, good. Okay."

Deputy Chief Finnegan came into the back. "Julie, I'm supposed to take you home."

"Okay, yeah, wait. I have another forty-five minutes."

"Stop, we'll be fine," Anna said. "High-school kids are coming in for the dinner shift. They can finish all this." She motioned to the sink of dishes.

"You sure?"

"Go home," Lew called across the grill. "And thanks."

Scott escorted Julie out the back and got into his squad car.

"How was he, the ferry guy? Did he give you any trouble?" she asked.

"None at all. He was almost too polite."

"After you drop me off you'll go back to the station to check on Morgan, right?"

"Yes, ma'am."

"Good."

The dream she'd had about Morgan, the one where he was shot and bleeding to death, twisted her insides into knots. She reminded herself that Morgan was a cop, the top cop of Port Whisper. She had faith in his abilities.

And then, a different kind of faith eased its way into her heart.

*God, if You're listening...*

The man from the ferry, Rick McDonald, sat across the table from Morgan in a conference room, wearing a stone-cold expression on his angular face. Rick didn't like being questioned. He probably figured he'd been cooperative, given Morgan his driver's license, showed him his P.I card. Rick had surrendered his firearm. Morgan's neck muscles tightened at the thought of him carrying it when he'd followed Julie onto the ferry.

If the guy wanted to be released anytime soon, he'd have to share the identity of his employer and purpose of this investigation.

"Why are you looking for Julie Burns?" Morgan said.

"Confidential."

"Tough. Her life has been threatened and you're my number-one suspect. You were stalking her on the ferry, and now you're in Port Whisper. Why?"

"I'd have to get permission from my—"

"Okay, lockup's down the hall." Morgan stood and pulled out his cuffs.

"Hang on, hang on."

Morgan waited.

"My client is a parent looking for her son. Julie Burns was his caseworker. The boy won't come back home and my job is to find him and bring him back."

"Why follow Julie onto the ferry?"

"I saw her take files with her from work. I was set up across the street with a telescopic lens. I figured if I could get the files, I could find out which flophouse the kid was living in."

"Why didn't you make an appointment with her at work and ask?"

"The kid's mother tried that. Julie wouldn't tell her anything."

"Wouldn't or didn't know?"

"You don't know the Windemeres. They get what they want. And they've got money to buy anything they want. Thea Windemere was convinced that Julie Burns knew more than she was sharing. It was my job to track her down and have a little chat."

"You mean threaten her?"

Rick shrugged. "I'm not into abusing women."

"Uh-huh. Why did it take you five days to get here?"

"I was distracted."

"You mean you couldn't successfully tail us."

"Windemere isn't my only client."

The guy didn't want to admit Morgan had done a good job of losing him once he got off the ferry. Rick had probably headed south toward Silverdale, instead of north.

"Are you going to let me talk to her?" the P.I. asked.

"Perhaps, if you check out. In the meantime, we've got a nice cell for you."

"Come on, man, a cell?"

"Yep."

"What's the deal with this girl?"

"What do you mean?"

"She must be into something pretty bad for you to assume I was sent to hurt her."

"The sooner we get you in the cell, the sooner I can do my background check, Rick."

"Okay, okay." He stood and Morgan led him to the town's one and only cell.

After locking Rick up, Morgan got to work. He started with a call to Ethan.

"Detective Beck."

"E, it's Morgan."

"It's been quiet on our end. No sightings of the Simms kid."

"We had a little excitement here. Someone came looking for Julie. I've locked him up while

I check him out. He's a P.I. who claims to be working for a concerned parent of a street kid."

"That's a twist."

"Can you do some checking on your end? His name is Rick McDonald."

Morgan gave Ethan Rick's birth date and driver's license number to help determine if the guy was legit.

"I'll get back to you," Ethan said.

"Thanks." Morgan hung up just as Scott walked into the office.

"You'd better call Julie and let her know you're okay," Scott said.

"Why wouldn't I be?"

"She was freaking out that the guy might attack you or something."

"She worries too much."

"About you, yeah." Scott winked at Morgan.

"Not you, too." Morgan turned to his computer.

"Can't help it. The whole town's rooting for you."

"The whole town should stay out of it." He didn't want idle gossip to interfere with their focus.

"Speaking of which, what time is the Community Cares meeting?"

"Seven. You coming?"

"Yeah, after my shift's over."

"Good, I could use the backup. I want to make sure they know their boundaries. I don't want to put civilians in danger."

"You afraid Scooner is going to dust off his shotgun and go trolling for bad guys?" Scott smiled.

"Wouldn't surprise me."

Morgan's phone rang and he picked up. "Chief Wright."

"Thank God you're okay," Julie said.

"As I was just saying to Scott, you worry too much."

"I'm conditioned to worry, remember? What's the deal with the ferry guy?"

"Claims to be a P.I. hired to ask you questions about one of your clients. You know a kid named Windemere?"

"Kurt, sure."

"His mom hired the P.I. to track you down. She's worried about her son."

"Worried? She disowned him when he was sixteen."

"That's his story. Sounds like she's got another."

"Do you need me to come down and talk to the investigator?"

"Not right now. I'm waiting to see if he checks out."

"What can I do?"

"Relax."

"Very funny."

"What, I thought you'd be exhausted after spending an afternoon washing dishes."

"I'm hyper."

"There's an Exercycle in the basement."

"Gee, thanks. Mom's expecting you for dinner at five-thirty."

"See you then."

Before they headed to the Community Cares meeting, Morgan took Julie by the police station to meet with Rick McDonald. He checked out, was a former Oregon cop with an exemplary record. Morgan just wished the guy would have stopped by the P.D. to officially inquire about Julie, which would have avoided a lot of drama.

Julie shared information about Kurt Windemere, his latest whereabouts, his job prospects and educational plans, yet Morgan sensed she was holding back.

She was protective of her kids, and rightfully so. Their biggest challenge was having an honest advocate in their corner to fight for them.

Morgan asked Rick not to reveal Julie's location, and if he couldn't make that promise, Morgan would find something to charge him with. Rick agreed and left town, but not before getting Julie's cell number in case he had more questions.

She seemed quiet as they drove to Evergreen Church on the outskirts of town for the meeting.

"Something bothering you?" he asked.

"Just thinking about Kurt. He's a good kid with really nutty parents. I mean, the mom sends a P.I. to find him, yet she kicked him out in the first place. I wonder if there's money involved."

"Money? How?"

"Perhaps Kurt is coming into a trust fund or something."

"My, aren't you cynical?"

"Can't help it. The woman does a complete one-eighty? Kicks him out, then wants him back? Makes no sense. That kind of volatile behavior contributes to the boys' life choices. They learn they can't trust anyone or anything."

"They trust you."

"Yeah, well, I work hard to earn that trust. And now…" Her voice trailed off.

"Now?"

"I've abandoned them."

"No, you just didn't abandon yourself."

She eyed him.

"Look," he started. "If you'd stayed back in Seattle for the kids, you would have put yourself in danger. That's self-abandonment in my book."

"I guess."

Morgan pulled into the church lot and scanned the property. He opened Julie's door and offered his hand. "Ready?"

"Yep."

They approached the church and Morgan's father's neighbor Anderson Green greeted them at the door.

"Anderson, do you remember Julie Burns?"

"Of course. Good to see you again, Julie." They shook hands.

"Thanks," Julie said.

"Come on in. The meeting will start in about ten minutes."

The mayor came up behind them, and Morgan motioned Julie down a hallway to the community room where a dozen people circled a long conference table. Edith had gotten a ride earlier with Caroline so they could set up refreshments. Anna, Wendy, Adeline Franks and Scooner Locke sat on one side of the table. They all welcomed Julie with greetings and warm smiles. Morgan noticed an odd look on her face. A look he'd never seen before.

"Grab some coffee and cookies," Wendy suggested.

"Thanks." Julie wandered to the refreshment

table and Morgan followed, sticking close. He didn't like being far away. He found it difficult to leave her at the restaurant or even at Dad's house.

That's why he planned to ask the mayor for a temporary leave, just until Julie's situation was resolved. Scott was more than able to take over for a week or two, and the town's other officers could cover Scott's shifts if he got bogged down in administrative duties. Besides, Morgan would be around. It wasn't as if he was going anywhere.

Although the thought had bounced around in his brain: What if Julie did agree to give their relationship another try? Could Morgan leave Port Whisper to be with her?

"Lana here yet?" Julie asked her mom.

"Not yet." Edith handed Julie an overloaded plate of cookies.

Julie smiled at Morgan. "You'd better help me with these."

"How generous of you." He led her to the table and they sat down. As he reached out to grab a cookie, their fingers touched.

"Sorry," he said. "Go ahead."

"No, you go. I shouldn't be eating any of this."

Morgan grabbed a chocolate-chip-bacon cookie and took a bite. He must have moaned because Julie nudged him.

"That good, huh?"

Sitting here eating cookies next to this beautiful woman? It was amazing.

"Yep" was all he could say.

Sketch appeared out of nowhere and sat next to Morgan. "Okay if I sit here?"

"Sure," Morgan said. "Where'd you come from?"

"Gran brought me along to help unload." Sketch scanned the room.

"Looking for someone?" Morgan said.

"Just doing a head count," Sketch answered.

"She's with Lana," Julie said.

Sketch whipped his attention to her. "Who?"

"Ashley. Or were you looking for someone else?"

"I wasn't looking for anyone." Sketch opened his laptop and pressed the power button. A screen saver of dancing monkeys popped up.

"Nice," Morgan said.

Sketch shrugged. Julie was right: the kid needed someone, an older-brother type, to help him navigate his way through the next few years. Morgan had warmed to the idea, realizing that although he'd have to put up with major attitude, the kid had a good heart. He wasn't motivated by malicious intent when he put the virus on the mechanic's computer. He did it because he felt his grandmother had been taken advantage of.

Now, if Morgan could just redirect Sketch's energy toward something productive.

"Have you got a map program on that computer of yours?" Morgan said.

"Yeah, why?"

"I thought you could create a map of town and pinpoint active neighborhood-watch groups. That would give us an idea of what parts of town are most vulnerable."

"Right on." Sketch got to work.

Julie touched Morgan's arm. "Good idea." She winked, and he understood she meant both a good idea for practical purposes, and for involving Sketch.

Morgan had noticed a few disapproving glances when Sketch walked in and sat next to him. People believed what they'd been told, unless you changed their minds. In this case, they believed Sketch was a troublemaker, probably because he didn't attend school, and he'd breached the mechanic's computer. There were a few other minor incidents Morgan had heard about: the Riscke boy got hurt in a tangle with Sketch, and Sketch had been out skateboarding after curfew, frightening Mrs. Critter into calling 9-1-1.

Hopefully after Sketch's participation in

this project, people would change their minds about him.

"I'm calling the Community Cares meeting to order at seven-twelve," Anderson announced from the head of the table. Mayor Davis had positioned himself next to Anderson in an authoritative move.

"We have one major item on our agenda this evening and that's strengthening our neighborhood-watch efforts to protect one of our own—Julie Burns."

The group glanced at Julie, and Morgan could sense her trepidation.

"As most of you know, she's been living in Seattle for the past ten years, working with street kids for Teen Life. Chief, do you want to explain what's going on?"

"Sure. Basically, someone has been threatening Julie and she came back to Port Whisper for support and protection. We're actively trying to discern who is after her and what the motivation is."

"How dangerous is this?" Adeline asked.

"We're not sure," Morgan said. "Whoever it is seems to want Julie for some mysterious reason, but I doubt anyone else is in danger."

"But you can't guarantee that, can you?" Mayor Davis interjected.

"No, sir."

"Which begs the question, why did she come back here if she knew she'd bring trouble with her?" the mayor pressed.

"I didn't think my stalker would follow me, or I never would have returned," Julie defended.

"Why didn't you go to the police?" Mayor Davis pushed.

"I did. They couldn't do anything about a crime that hadn't been committed yet."

"Where would you go if you were a young woman in Seattle being stalked?" Wendy challenged the mayor.

"I wouldn't involve innocent people in my drama."

"Last time I checked, Port Whisper was about community," Scooner said. "Our group is called Community Cares, remember?"

The group broke out into conversation.

"Okay, everyone take a breath," Anderson directed. "Instead of focusing on the problem, let's focus on the solution. We need to contact our neighborhood-watch captains and fill them in. Spread the word about what's going on. Julie, are you comfortable with that?"

"What are you going to tell them?"

"That a stalker's after you and it's our job to protect you."

"Okay, sure."

Sketch raised his hand.

"Yes, young man?" Anderson said.

Sketch flipped his laptop around so everyone could see the screen. "I've mapped out the town and highlighted neighborhood-watch areas. We could strengthen involvement between Fourth and Jensen up to Wellington, and on the south end from Cherry and Main, west to Edlund Avenue." Sketch glanced up. The group was staring at him. "That's my suggestion, anyway."

He turned his laptop around and fidgeted in his chair.

"Thank you, Sketch," Anderson said. "Great work. Who is closest to those areas?"

Wendy and Adeline raised their hands.

"Would you ladies like to talk to your groups about expanding, perhaps offering an incentive for neighborhoods to join the watch team?"

"Sure." Adeline leaned toward Wendy. "We'll talk after the meeting."

"Chief, what specifically should we be looking for?" Anderson asked.

"Anyone you don't recognize, or if you see questionable behavior. Do not approach them, but keep watch and call 9-1-1. By all means, trust your fear sense. That prickling sensation on the back of your neck? It happens for a reason."

The door to the community room burst open

and Ashley ran inside. She was visibly shaken, flushed and out of breath.

Sketch rushed to her and put his arm around her shoulder.

"Ashley, what's wrong?" Morgan stood.

"I didn't… She said…"

"Ashley, take a deep breath," Morgan coached. "What happened?"

"I was supposed to meet her at the office and…and I got there and the door was unlocked so I went in and the place was trashed, and… and Lana's gone!"

# Chapter Twelve

Morgan quickly took charge to prevent the group from spiraling out of control.

"Everyone focus on your responsibilities—notifying your neighborhood-watch members, helping Wendy and Adeline reach out to the weaker districts. Sketch, you can help with that. Scooner?"

Scooner stood. "Yes, Chief."

"I'm counting on you to speak personally with our local business owners. It's important that they pay extra attention to strangers in the area, especially tourists who ask a lot of questions, but don't seem all that interested in buying anything in the store.

"Caroline, take Edith back to my dad's place." Morgan cast a glance at the group. "Stay calm and don't overreact. I will email you all with an update when I find Lana. Ashley? I need to speak to you outside."

With a resigned nod, Ashley and Sketch walked toward the front door. Julie followed, but Morgan put out his hand. "I really need you to keep things cool in here. Julie, you're a counselor. Put those skills to work."

"But it's my sister," she whispered.

"Pretend it's someone else's sister, just for now. These folks are going to take their lead from us. The more upset we are, the less they'll be able to think rationally. Sketch, give me five minutes alone with Ashley, then she's all yours, okay?"

Sketch nodded. "Five and I'm coming out."

Morgan led Ashley outside and called Scott, alerting him to the development. Scott said he'd meet Morgan at the scene, Lana's snack shop.

Morgan turned his full attention back to Ashley. "Okay, tell me exactly what Lana said about meeting her."

"She said to meet at six, that we'd have dinner and come over here. But I was at Jenni's and lost track of time and…and…"

"Calm down, take a deep breath. Did she have an evening tour? The boat could have broken down."

"She had a holiday tour at four, but she was supposed to be back by five-thirty."

"Did you notice if the boat was gone?"

"No, I was so freaked I ran straight here."

"Why didn't you call 9-1-1?"

"I knew you'd be here and... Sketch."

"Okay, close your eyes and tell me what the office looked like when you went inside."

She nodded and closed her eyes. "I knocked a few times, but when she didn't answer I tried the door. I figured she'd left it open for me. The lights were on. Paperwork was all over the place and her chair was tipped over."

"What about her purse? Keys?"

Ashley's eyes popped open. "Her backpack was on the floor. She doesn't carry a purse, but she doesn't go anywhere without her pack. Oh, do you think someone—"

"Let's focus on finding her."

"I feel bad, like it's my fault, like I did something wrong."

"You didn't. You did great. You got help."

She nodded and the door whipped open. Sketch ran to Ashley and hugged her.

"Sorry," he said to Morgan, "I couldn't wait."

"No problem. Make sure she gets home."

Morgan went back inside and motioned to Julie. She joined him outside and they got into his truck.

"I'll take you home," he said.

"No. I'm coming with you."

Pulling out of the lot, he said, "This is unwise."

"It's my sister, Morgan. I'm not running anymore."

Morgan's cell rang and he hit the speakerphone. "Chief Wright."

"It's Scott. The place is trashed, all right, but I can't tell if anything's missing."

"And the boat?"

"Haven't checked yet. I'm still in the office."

"Julie and I will be there in a minute."

Morgan ended the call and eyed Julie. "Don't worry, your sister's a black belt. They're probably going to be sorry they messed with her in the first place. That's to say, if anyone has messed with her."

"What do you mean?"

"She could have just taken off, forgotten something and had to run out or—"

"Her office was trashed, Morgan, but thanks for trying."

They found a parking spot in front of Stone Soup. Julie raced into the office, while Morgan marched toward the water. The dock was empty, which meant someone had stolen her boat and taken her with them or she'd decided on a night tour for her own personal enjoyment. Wishful thinking.

The most likely scenario was that someone

had taken both Lana and the boat. Which meant a ransom call should be expected.

Scott and Julie came outside.

"The boat's gone," Morgan said.

Suddenly Julie's phone rang. "Hello?"

"Julie, it's Lana."

"Where are you? We've been worried—"

"My cell signal is weak…had to…idiot…failure…and…someone's here."

"Where, here?"

"On…island…"

The line went dead. "Lana!"

Turning to Morgan she said, "I think she's on Sahalish Island. She was breaking up. But she said 'someone's here.' We gotta get over there."

"Maybe we can get a Coast Guard cruiser to help us out," Scott suggested.

"It'll take too long," Morgan said.

"Chief!" Scooner said rushing up to the dock out of breath. "What's the status?"

"We think Lana's stuck on Sahalish Island."

"Let's go." Scooner motioned them toward his slip.

"I don't like involving civilians," Morgan said.

"I was a Navy SEAL. Don't think of myself as a civilian. Come on."

Morgan wanted to order Julie to stay back, but he knew she'd refuse. Besides, if she stayed back, who would protect her?

They climbed aboard Scooner's boat and Julie squeezed Morgan's hand, her eyes filling with anguish.

"It'll be okay, honey," he said, and hugged her.

Scooner took off for the island and Morgan wrapped his arm around Julie's shoulder, holding her close. What was only a fifteen-minute ride seemed to take hours. The closer they got, the more tension he felt drifting off Julie's body.

She was leaning into him and it felt right, more right than any connection he'd felt to another woman.

He refused to believe it was transference. This connection was a lot more than a woman being vulnerable and depending emotionally on her protector.

Morgan played out in his head what would happen once they got there: he'd leave Julie with Scooner on the boat while he and Scott searched for Lana. Julie wouldn't be happy with that decision, but he couldn't worry about what would make her happy.

He was committed to what would keep her safe.

Being former military, Scooner was no stranger to firearms. If he didn't have one on the boat, Morgan would loan him his second piece, currently tucked away in his ankle holster. Some would think the second firearm was overkill for a small town, but old habits died hard, and it was habit from working in a bigger law-enforcement agency.

They pulled up on the other side of the dock from Lana's boat.

"Scooner, you packin'?" Morgan asked.

"Yes, sir."

Scott and Morgan hopped off, then tied up the boat. "Julie, you stay back with Scooner."

"But—"

"No arguments," Morgan interrupted her, then looked at Scooner. "I'm depending on you to protect her."

"Will do, Chief."

"Let's go," Morgan said to Scott.

"Morgan, wait."

He glanced over his shoulder. She looked at him with pleading eyes. He got the message: be careful.

"We'll be right back," Morgan said.

They headed up the trail, scanning the surrounding woods. Morgan pulled out his flashlight to illuminate the path in front of them.

"Think we should call out her name?" Scott asked.

"No. She may not be alone."

They climbed up the trail to an overlook, giving them a complete view of the island. Although it was night, the full moon lit the surrounding area, giving Morgan and Scott a clear view of the west side of the island.

"Well, we know she's here," Scott said.

The sound of a motor echoed from the east side of the island.

"Let's go," Morgan said.

Pulling out his gun, he and Scott raced down the trail through a heavily wooded area to the other side. Just as they hit a clearing, Morgan spotted a boat speeding off.

"Think they've got her?" Scott said.

"Help!" a female voice echoed from behind them.

Morgan and Scott spun around.

"Lana!" Morgan called out.

"Where's it coming from?" Scott said.

"Somebody, help me!"

"Back this way," Morgan said.

They rushed back into the woods. "Lana, keep calling out so we can find you!" Scott yelled.

"By the Quinault rock!"

Morgan knew that landmark and its history. "Come on," he directed Scott and raced to the rock, heart racing, brain spinning.

They burst out of the woods and Morgan could see the Quinault rock a hundred feet away. But no Lana.

"Lana!" he called.

"Down here!"

"Other side of the rock," Scott said.

They sprinted and Morgan grabbed Scott just before he fell into an opening in the ground.

"What the…?" Scott said.

They peered over the edge into a five-foot hole. Morgan aimed his flashlight down below and spotted Lana, face smudged, knees hugged to her chest.

"I fell in a hole. I'm an idiot."

Morgan holstered his gun and handed the flashlight to Scott. Kneeling, Morgan reached down for Lana. "Give me your hand."

"All right, give me a sec to stand up. I think I sprained my ankle."

"Take your time," Morgan said. Relief surged through his body. So, this wasn't related to Julie's situation. Yet who was the guy in the motorboat? He'd deal with that later.

"Ow, ow, ow," Lana said, wobbling on one foot while babying the other. "Okay, ready."

Morgan reached down, gripped her hand and pulled. Scott kneeled beside him and grabbed Lana by the belt and together they hoisted her to safety.

She collapsed on her back. "Man, am I glad to see you guys."

"What happened?" Morgan asked, as Scott helped her stand.

"I couldn't find Edgar, my phone, and I needed it for tomorrow. I remembered the last place I saw it was on the island, so I came back to find it."

"Your office was a mess."

Lana nibbled at her lower lip. "Ah, I'm so embarrassed. I had a tantrum."

Scott eyed her.

"I was frustrated because I couldn't find my phone and knew I was forgetting something," she continued. "I know, immature."

With an arm behind her knees, Morgan picked her up and carried her down the trail.

"Ooooh, Julie's gonna be jealous."

"How did you fall into the hole?" Morgan redirected.

"It's stupid, really."

"Tell me anyway."

"I thought I heard something and got spooked. You'd think I'd be used to the sounds of wildlife by now. Anyway, I took off running and didn't see the hole. I mean, what kind of animal digs a five-foot hole?"

"Lana!" Julie cried out, running up the wooden dock. "What happened?"

"I fell. I'm fine. I think I sprained my ankle."

Morgan set her safely into the tour boat. "I'll drive Lana's boat back to Port Whisper and take her to the emergency room."

"I'm coming with you," Julie said, then turned to Scooner. "Thank you so much."

"My pleasure."

"I'll ride with Scooner," Scott said.

Morgan untied Lana's boat, got aboard and headed for Port Whisper.

"What were you thinking coming out here in the dark?" Julie said.

"Hey, it's a full moon. It's not that bad. And I needed my phone. It's my brain."

As the sisters talked about the evening's events—the Community Cares meeting and Lana's mishap on the island—Morgan couldn't get the sound of the motorboat out of his mind. He could rationalize someone coming out to fish, but a visit to the island at night? It didn't make sense. Had someone followed Lana to the island in the hopes of taking her hostage to get at Julie?

He'd add that to the list of things to investigate.

"I was so freaked out," Julie said. "I hated waiting on the boat with Scooner while Morgan and Scott went to find you. I felt so helpless and all I could do was…" Her voice trailed off.

"What?" Lana rubbed Julie's shoulder.

"I found myself praying."

"Well, it worked." Lana smiled and hugged her sister.

Morgan focused on the nighttime lights of

Port Whisper as his heart flooded with hope. She prayed for her sister. Julie had come to Port Whisper a woman without faith. Morgan said a silent prayer of thanks, for opening her heart to God.

Julie stayed close to her sister during the examination and diagnosis of her ankle. It was a bad sprain and she'd have to use crutches, but it could have been so much worse. They decided to take Lana back to Morgan's dad's house and have her sleep on the couch so Julie and Mom could take care of her.

Morgan was unusually quiet, and the next morning she decided to ask what was bothering him. She wandered into the kitchen where Mom made breakfast.

"Good morning." Julie gave her mother a hug.

"How'd you sleep, sweetie?"

"Pretty good, considering."

"A lot of excitement last night."

"More than I'm used to. Where's Lana?"

"Up and gone already. Can you believe it? She was determined to open the snack shop."

"Her ankle must be hurting."

"She doesn't show it."

Julie admired her sister for not missing a beat, for her determination not to let anything throw her off track. It inspired her to refocus on her own situation to discover who was threatening her and how to stop it.

"Where's Morgan?" Julie asked.

"Went to check in at work. He'll be back. Wouldn't miss cinnamon French toast."

Mom and Julie sat down to breakfast. It amazed Julie how the taste of Mom's cooking could make everything right. Home. Family. She realized how much she'd missed this feeling in the past ten years.

A few minutes later Morgan came into the kitchen.

"Ladies," he greeted.

"Morgan, let me fix you a plate." Mom stood.

"I'll get it," he said.

"Nonsense. Sit down and talk to us."

Morgan sat down next to Julie and Mom slid a plate of French toast in front of him, along with a mug of hot coffee. "Busy morning already?"

"Just wrapping some things up."

"Wrapping up?" Julie asked.

"Work stuff, boring."

Julie sensed something was up.

"Well, I'd better change into my work clothes," Mom said. "Caroline's coming over and we're starting on the kitchen. I hope you trust us, Morgan."

"You've done great work on the living room so far."

"I'm glad you like it. And after the kitchen we're going to decorate for Christmas, so either you tell us where the decorations are or we'll all pitch in and use our own."

Morgan sighed. "You win. There are two boxes marked Christmas out in the garage by the workbench."

"Perfect." Mom left them alone and Julie turned to Morgan.

"What's going on? You seemed, I don't know, unusually quiet last night."

Morgan put down his fork. "A few things concern me about the events of last night. Mostly the motorboat Scott and I heard speeding away from the island. It's unusual for someone to be out there at night."

"You think it's related to my case?"

"Not sure. Scott and I went back early this morning to check things out. The hole your sister fell into had been camouflaged, which is why she didn't see it."

"Was there anything down there?"

"No, which is even more puzzling. I've contacted the Feds. My gut tells me this could be related to smuggling something in from Canada, storing it on the island temporarily, then distributing it." His phone rang and Morgan picked up. "Hey, Scott. Yep…try the bottom drawer of the file cabinet. Don't worry about that now. You need to focus on administrative tasks. Yep, anytime."

"What was that about?" Julie said.

Morgan sighed and leaned back in his chair. Julie didn't like this expression. She sensed he was preparing to give her bad news.

"Morgan?"

"The way the grapevine works in this town, you're going to find out soon enough." He shot her a serious look. "I'm taking a temporary leave of absence and Scott's taking over."

Julie leaned forward. "What? Why?"

"The mayor's been on my case, and he's right—I'm distracted. It's best that I hand the reins over to someone else for a little while."

"Morgan, you can't—"

"It's done."

"Because of me. No, I won't be responsible for you losing your job." She stood and paced the kitchen.

Morgan got up and went to her, but she continued her pace to keep a safe distance between them.

"I'm not losing my job. I'm just stepping back for a few weeks. I've been considering a leave since Dad was hospitalized. It's not a new concept for me."

She pulled away from him. "See, this is exactly what I didn't want to happen. I've messed up your life, your dream. It's not right."

"It's what I need to do right now. You are my priority."

"I'm just going to hurt you again, ruin your career and abandon you."

Morgan took her hand and pulled her close. "Are you, Julie, really?"

He leaned forward and kissed her. A gentle, sweet kiss that made her want to cry. It felt so right to be held like this, to be kissed with such tenderness. She wanted to break away, to tell him he was making a huge mistake, but something stopped her. She was enjoying the kiss a little too much.

Suddenly her phone rang. He broke the kiss and looked into her eyes. "You'd better answer that. Your sister might need you."

Gathering her thoughts, she went to her purse and pulled out the phone. "Hello?"

"Miss Burns! They're gonna kill me!"

# *Chapter Thirteen*

"Who is this?"

"Dane. I escaped but they got Andy and now they're after me."

"How did you get this number?"

"From Mr. Pratt."

She gripped the phone tighter. "Where are you?"

"Seattle, north side."

"It's Dane," she told Morgan.

"Have him call Ethan."

"Dane, call Detective Ethan Beck. I'll give you his—"

"No, no cops! They'll kill Andy."

"But—"

"Help me, you gotta help."

"Can you get to the Edmonds Ferry?"

"Yeah, I think so."

"Take the ferry over to Kingston and we'll pick you up."

Morgan waved her off, but she ignored him. Dane was calling for help. She wouldn't turn him away.

"I'm so scared," he croaked.

"Take a deep breath. Focus on catching a bus to the ferry terminal. You'll get to Kingston before us, so just wait in the park."

"I'm sorry, I'm so sorry. I didn't mean to get you involved in this."

"In what? What is this about?"

"I gotta go."

"Dane? Dane!"

Silence echoed back at her. Julie sighed, beating back the worry in her chest.

"I wish you hadn't told him to take the ferry," Morgan said.

"You should have heard him. He was out of his mind, terrified. What was I supposed to do?"

"It could be a setup. Whoever is after you could have enlisted the boy's help to find you."

"Dane would never do that. He's in trouble and has no one to turn to. It's my responsibility to make sure he's okay."

"What did he say, exactly?"

"That he'd escaped, but he didn't say from where."

"But he wouldn't speak with Ethan?"

"He's doesn't trust cops."

"Because he's into something illegal?"

"Enough with the twenty questions. We need to meet him at the ferry."

"Go tell your mom what's going on and I'll call Ethan."

She kissed his cheek. "Thanks."


Three hours later Morgan found street parking near the ferry and Julie flung open her door. Morgan placed his hand on her shoulder.

"Hang on. We need to be ready in case it's a setup."

"Morgan, I told you—"

"Jules, I know you believe in this kid, but the reality is even if he isn't a part of a trap, whoever is after him could have followed him onto the ferry. Can you just trust me?"

She nodded in agreement, but he could tell she was distracted, worried about the boy's safety.

"There's a coffee shop on the corner," Morgan started. "I'll set you up there while I check out the park. You can see everything from the coffee shop. I'll search for Dane, and when I identify him, you give me the thumbs-up sign. But you stay back. Do not expose yourself. I'll try and convince him to come back to the car with me."

"He won't trust you, Morgan. You're a stranger and he's frightened."

"Let me worry about that, okay?"

He got out of the car and came around to open her door. Motioning her out, he scanned the area for signs of danger. All clear. He led her to the coffee shop.

"There are plenty of people around. You'll be safe in here."

With a nod, she went into the shop and found a spot at the counter overlooking the park.

Morgan crossed the street, continuing to survey the surrounding area. This was the perfect opportunity to flush Julie out of her hiding spot. Using the kid as bait made sense, yet all Julie could focus on was helping Dane.

Morgan admired that about her, her dedication to her job and helping the kids. But Morgan had to teach her to draw the line when it came to sacrificing her safety for another's.

He searched the park for both Dane and any sign of danger. It was a sunny, yet chilly December morning, so there weren't many people wandering around. Probably a good thing, since Morgan didn't want an audience. If Dane refused to go with him, Morgan might have to use gentle force.

More commuters were filing down the ferry ramp, yet Dane should have been here by now.

Morgan scoped out the park, but didn't see any teenage boys, so he walked up to the ticket booth and flashed his badge.

"Did you happen to see a young man, about seventeen, get off the ferry in the last few hours? Maybe he looked nervous or confused?"

"Actually, yeah, a kid like that wandered around for a while. When a police car cruised past, he took off."

"Which direction?"

"Down, toward the water."

"Thanks."

Morgan walked through the park and motioned to Julie to stay put. The kid was probably looking for a place to hide from authorities, which only confirmed Morgan's suspicions that he'd broken the law.

Morgan flipped his jacket collar up against the chill and headed down to the rocky shore. As he got closer to the water, he glanced beneath the pylons and spotted a young man hugging his knees, his head buried in his arms, sitting on a large boulder.

"Dane?"

The kid jumped to his feet. "Who are you?"

"Julie sent me."

"I don't believe you." Dane whipped a knife out of his pocket.

"Hey, kid, relax. I'm Julie's friend and she sent me to get you."

"Why didn't she come?"

"She's here, waiting for you in a coffee shop on the corner. I didn't want to expose her and put her in danger in case you were followed."

"I wasn't, unless you're with them."

"I'm not. I live in Port Whisper and Julie and I used to be friends in high school."

"Prove it, show me your license."

Morgan pulled out his wallet to slip out his license.

"Wait." The kid backed up. "That's a badge. You're a cop! Get away or I'll cut you, I will."

"Then I'd have to arrest you and none of us want that, especially not Julie."

"I don't believe you!" he shouted.

"Dane?" Julie said from behind Morgan.

"Jules, I told you to stay back," Morgan said.

"Dane, put down the knife. Please? Morgan's my friend."

"He's a cop. Why'd you bring a cop?"

"He's my friend who happens to be a cop. Now put it away so we can take you someplace safe."

"He's gonna arrest me."

"No, he's not, are you, Morgan?"

He could. He could charge the kid with threatening a police officer, for starters.

"We just want to help you, Dane. I'm not going to arrest you," Morgan assured.

Dane hesitated, as if debating if he should run, or take Julie and Morgan at their word.

"Come on, drop the knife so we can go home. We've got a great place for you to stay, a comfortable bed and awesome home-cooked meals. Please, Dane?" Julie pleaded.

Dane dropped the knife and took a few steps toward Morgan and Julie.

And collapsed.

"Dane!" Julie cried out. She and Morgan rushed to either side of him. Morgan felt for his pulse.

"It's racing. We need to get him to a hospital," Morgan said.

"What do you think's wrong?"

"Could be any number of things." Morgan stood and made the 9-1-1 call.

"Come on, Dane, wake up. It's okay. I'm here. You're safe," Julie encouraged.

The desperation in her voice tangled Morgan's gut into a knot as he gave their location to the dispatch operator. Morgan hated to think how disappointed she'd be if Dane was passed out from a drug overdose. She believed so strongly in the boy's determination to kick drugs and live a productive life.

"They should be here soon," Morgan said, kneeling beside Dane. "Jules?"

She glanced up. "I know, I know, I shouldn't have come down here."

"What I was going to say was, keep a positive attitude. The boy's young and strong. If you're right and he's been off drugs for a while, it could be dehydration, or exhaustion from running."

"Why are they after him?" she croaked. "Isn't it hard enough to battle an addiction on your own without someone chasing you around for… for what?"

Morgan placed his hand over hers, splayed across Dane's back. "We'll figure it out. I promise."

"He's a good boy, Morgan, and he deserves better."

"Then have faith that he'll be okay."

Luckily it wasn't too busy at Memorial Hospital when they brought Dane into the emergency room. Still, it seemed to be taking forever for someone to update Julie and Morgan on Dane's condition. It had been five hours of waiting and worrying.

Julie got up and paced the waiting area, a bundle of nervous energy.

"Jules, relax," Morgan said.

"Why is it taking so long?"

Morgan stood and took her hand. "They'll talk to us when they know something. They probably don't want to guess at this point."

She realized she instantly felt better from the connection of their hands. Morgan grounded her, calmed her racing heart.

"I'm too wound up to sit," she said, pulling away from him.

Depending on Morgan's touch was a dangerous habit to embrace. He wouldn't be around once this case was over and then what would she do?

The E.R. door burst open and a doctor approached them.

"How is he?" she asked before the doctor could speak.

"Dehydrated. We have him on fluids, but it would help to know what else is in his system. Do you know if he's on any medications or if he's been taking any drugs?"

"No, I don't," she said. "Did you ask him?"

"He's in and out, not very lucid yet. In a few hours he'll be up to answering some questions."

"Questions?"

"About what he's on."

"You're assuming he's on drugs?" Even she couldn't miss the accusation in her voice.

"Something caused these symptoms besides

dehydration. We've sent his blood work to the lab to figure it out."

"Thanks, Doctor," Morgan said.

With a nod, the doctor went back into the E.R.

"He's not abusing drugs, Morgan. I know it in my heart."

"One thing at a time, sweetheart. He's in good hands and he's okay for now. That's good news."

Just then Morgan's cell rang. "I'm going to take this outside. You stay right here, okay?"

"Sure." She flopped down in a vinyl chair and stared at the television. Nothing kept her interest for long, not with the worry still eating away at her. Dane had to be okay. He just had to be.

She'd stay at his bedside until he was well enough to leave the hospital, and then she'd take him back to Port Whisper, where he'd be safe. Glancing around the waiting area, she realized it could have been much worse. Detective Beck could have called with the news that Dane had been found dead on some random street in Seattle.

*Be grateful that Dane made it across the water,* she reminded herself. But would he ultimately be okay?

She wasn't sure why, but she clasped her hands together and closed her eyes. She hadn't prayed like this in years, but she suddenly found herself in a place of surrender.

*Please, God, watch over Dane. He's a good boy who's tried to kick drugs and live a better life.*

As she pressed her hands together, she found herself letting go of the panic, the worry. She released it to God.

When she opened her eyes a few minutes later, Morgan was sitting next to her. He didn't ask what she'd been doing. He didn't have to.

"Hey," he said.

"Hi."

A silent understanding passed between them.

"Who was on the phone?" she asked.

"Ethan. We'll talk about it later. I've got Dane's room number. Want to head up there?"

"Yes."

As they walked to the elevators Morgan said, "I really admire your dedication and faith in Dane."

"Thanks."

"There aren't a lot of people who have seen what you've seen or gone through what you have who could still believe in someone so completely. Most people would have grown cynical beyond the ability to have faith."

"I have my days, for sure, but there's something about this kid that touches my heart. I feel

like I can help him dig his way out of the hole
he's dropped into. Know what I mean?"

"Yes, I do."

The elevator doors opened and he motioned
her inside.

"Having someone believe in you that much
can make all the difference," he said.

She wondered if they were talking about
Dane, or about Julie and Morgan. When they'd
first been teamed up in high-school biology for
a project, he had been angry and withdrawn.
She'd sensed his anger was a cover for pain,
and even at sixteen she'd instinctively reached
out to him. And was glad she had. He'd always
said her belief in him at a critical time in his
life had essentially saved him. His mother had
left Morgan and his dad. His dad, who'd had to
keep his anger bottled up in his role as police
chief, took out his rage on his son, leading Morgan to think his mother's absence was his fault.

A heavy load for a teenager.

Once she'd pushed past his defense barriers,
Julie had seen the wonderful qualities of Morgan Wright: his sense of humor, creative streak
and determination. Things that had lain dor-
mant until she'd come into his life. He'd said
it more than once when they'd dated. They'd
both said a lot of things as they planned their
future together.

Then Suzy had died and something changed in Julie's heart. She hadn't done enough for her friend and needed to make it right somehow, which is why she'd chosen to counsel lost kids. But who had she been making it up to? Suzy? God?

"Hey, the doctor said he's just dehydrated." Morgan squeezed her hand, thinking she'd been worrying about Dane.

"Thanks," she said.

They stepped off the elevator and headed to Dane's room. A nurse was getting him settled in.

"I'm sorry, could you wait outside?" the nurse said.

"No, I need her in here," Dane croaked. "Miss Burns, don't leave! Don't!"

The nurse motioned Julie into the room and Morgan hung back by the door, probably wanting to avoid upsetting Dane.

Julie leaned against the window ledge and watched as the nurse adjusted his IV and checked his blood pressure.

"A little better," she said, taking off the blood-pressure cuff. "The best thing you can do is rest." She glanced at Julie. "Try to keep him calm."

"Of course."

The nurse left and Julie pulled a chair up to Dane's bed. "How are you feeling?"

He shrugged.

"Dumb question, huh?" Julie joked.

"I'm scared."

She took his hand. "It's okay. You're safe here."

"I'm never safe."

"Are you up to telling us what this is about?"

"Us?"

"Morgan's protecting me, Dane, so he should know everything."

"I don't like cops."

"Make an exception. He's a good man." She glanced at Morgan in the doorway and he smiled.

"Okay, I guess," Dane said.

Morgan came into the room and stood at the foot of the bed. "Who is after you?"

"A guy named Henson. He works for some big drug company."

"Why is he after you?" Morgan pressed.

"We were testing out some drugs for him."

"We?"

"Me and Andy, and a few other guys. Henson and two guys in suits came up to us on the street and said they were developing a new drug to help addicts kick their drug habits. I thought, why not? Andy didn't want to…" Dane laid his head back on the pillow, his eyelids drooping.

"You should rest," Julie offered.

"No, I need to tell you…" He paused. "We tried the drugs, but instead of stopping the addiction, it made us hyper, like crazy. They wanted us to sell the drug to our friends, but Andy said no. That's when they took him."

"Took him where?"

Dane shrugged.

"Why do you think they took him?" Morgan asked.

"Because he threatened to…go to the cops." Dane struggled to keep his eyes open.

"Rest, Dane," Julie said.

"No, I have to…about Andy… Henson said if I kept dealing the drug he wouldn't hurt Andy, but if I didn't…it's my fault, it was my idea to test the drug. They paid us cash and I figured I wasn't hurting anyone." He paused. "I really messed up and now Andy—"

"Shh," Julie said, touching his hand. "Don't go there. You need to rest and get better."

"You'll stay?" he whispered.

"I'll be right here," she assured.

With a sigh, Dane closed his eyes and was out.

Julie held on to his hand and glanced at Morgan. "They're using these boys as guinea pigs. We've got to stop them, Morgan."

"I'll call Ethan. He might want to involve the DEA."

"I'd hate to think how many other boys are being targeted. We have to find Andy."

"Jules, can you step into the hallway with me for just a second?" Morgan asked.

"I told him I'd stay."

"Please."

The tone of his voice, the sudden seriousness of his blue-green eyes, sent a shiver down her spine.

"Morgan, what is it?"

He extended his hand and she took it. Morgan led her just outside Dane's hospital room door. "I talked to Ethan earlier," Morgan said, gently squeezing her hand. "I'm sorry. They found Andy's body this afternoon."

"His body—you mean…?"

"He's dead."

# Chapter Fourteen

Her golden eyes stared back at him with a mixture of disbelief and anger. Morgan positioned himself to grab her if her legs gave out.

"But we didn't identify the body," she said.

"Your work associate, William, did. They're calling it an accidental drug overdose."

Morgan studied her perplexed expression, wishing to God that he could offer appropriate comfort. More than anything, Morgan wanted to ease her pain.

"Dane is going to be devastated. He blames himself," she said.

"Don't tell him quite yet. Let's wait until he's feeling better."

"I need to convince him not to carry this burden. It's not his fault Andy was killed. Henson and his men are responsible."

"Absolutely."

"Dane thought he was doing the right thing by testing out a new drug and it backfired. We all make mistakes." She glanced into the open doorway. "I need to teach him self-forgiveness. But I'm worried, Morgan. This could be the stressor that sends him into a nosedive."

"Then you show him compassion and we surround him with people who care and want to help."

She fingered her silver locket and closed her eyes. The locket Andy gave her. "He was a good kid, just lost."

"We all get lost at one point or another," Morgan said.

"Even when we think we know where we're going."

"How are you feeling about Andy's death?"

"I'm sad, but honestly not surprised. I guess deep down I'd prepared myself for the possibility. He made some bad choices in the past. It was like he was addicted to the adrenaline rush of taking risks and avoiding the consequences. Still, I really thought I could help him."

"I'm sure you did. He gave you the locket because you were a special person in his life. Hold on to that."

She nodded.

"Miss Burns!" Dane called from the room.

"Go," Morgan said. "I'll be close."

With a nod she went into the boy's room and settled beside his bed, calming him with a touch of her hand. Morgan was confident she'd find a way to give him peace, show him that it wasn't his fault that his friend was killed. If only Julie could do the same for herself.

That was Morgan's goal, to open her eyes to her own sense of self-forgiveness.

Dane slept on and off throughout the night, with Julie by his side. The medical team felt confident that he was well enough to be released, and although Morgan wasn't completely comfortable with bringing Dane back to Port Whisper, the kid didn't have anyplace else to go.

The doctor told Morgan the blood-work results indicated something in Dane's system could have caused the dehydration, but they couldn't identify it. The mystery drug Henson was testing? The doctors couldn't be sure.

Julie finished up the paperwork and paid for the medical charges. She said it was the right thing to do. As they rode the elevator to Dane's floor she asked, "Did you speak with Ethan?"

"Yes. He's the lead on Andy's death investigation."

"You mean murder?"

"They're not calling it murder...yet."

"What did he say?" She fought back a yawn as they stepped off the elevator.

"He'd call when he had something solid. In the meantime, he notified the DEA about our mysterious Mr. Henson and his associates."

Julie stopped in the middle of the hallway and squared off at Morgan. "It's been a week and I don't feel like we're any closer to resolving this."

"Anxious to get back to work?"

Sadness colored her golden eyes and he wondered what'd he'd said to upset her. "Jules?"

"I want my life back, Morgan, and I want to put these creeps behind bars."

"Let's get Dane and head home." He took her hand and she didn't pull away. They held hands as they walked down the hallway to Dane's room.

He relished the feeling, the warmth of her fingers entwined with his. He'd enjoy this for as long as he could, still hoping, praying, that she'd give love another chance. With him.

They turned the corner into Dane's room.

The bed was empty.

"Dane?" she said. Her head spun around to eye the bathroom. The door was open. No one was inside. She pinned Morgan with panicked eyes.

"Come on." He led her to the nurses' station,

where a nurse was keying something into her computer. "Excuse me?"

The nurse glanced at Morgan.

"We're supposed to take Dane Simms home today, but he's not in his room. Is he with a doctor?"

"No, I don't think so."

A second nurse came out of a room and wandered up to the station.

"Paula, do you know where Dane Simms is?" she asked.

"The boy in 314?"

"Yes," Julie said.

"No, I haven't seen him since the doctor signed his discharge papers."

"I need to speak with security." Morgan flashed his badge.

The nurse behind the desk punched in a number and handed Morgan the phone. Julie pulled away from him, probably to search the floor.

"Nuh-uh." Morgan grabbed her arm. "You're staying right here with me."

"Security," a man said on the other end of the line.

"This is Morgan Wright. I'm the police chief in Port Whisper. A patient who's supposed to be released to me today is missing. I need your help locating him," Morgan said in a calm, controlled voice. He hoped his demeanor would calm Julie's panic.

"We don't have the staff to search the entire hospital, but I can put the word out that he's missing."

"Great." Morgan gave him Dane's description and asked to see the security tapes. The security officer agreed and Morgan led Julie into the elevator.

The doors closed and she paced the small space. "This means they're close, doesn't it? They found him. They took him," she said.

"We don't know that. Dane could have gone out for a walk, or gone to get something to eat."

She nodded, but he knew he hadn't convinced her. The doors opened and they headed toward security. Once there, Morgan asked to cue up video from that last hour on the third floor. He motioned Julie to a chair and stood behind her, placing his hands on her shoulders.

They watched the video for fifteen minutes until they spotted Dane coming out of his room. With a paranoid whip of his head, he looked both ways, then shot down the hall to the stairway.

Morgan's instincts went on full alert. The kid left on his own? Was this a setup to flush Julie out of hiding?

"Why would he leave like that? I told him we

were taking him someplace safe," Julie said, glancing over her shoulder at Morgan.

"Here's my cell number." He handed the security officer his card. "Call me if you see him."

"Will do."

Morgan motioned Julie out of the office. "We need to retrace his steps. See if he dropped something or left us any indication of what happened."

"He has to be okay, Morgan. He just has to be."

Anger flared in Morgan's chest at the possibility that the kid was part of a plan to find Julie. No, if Julie had faith in Dane, Morgan needed to follow her lead and give the kid the benefit of the doubt, as well.

They got to Dane's room and searched the floor, the bed and the closet. Nothing.

"Let's check the stairs," he said. Although he considered the threat to Julie if they found Dane with the man who set this up, Morgan couldn't leave her alone and vulnerable. Besides, she'd never let him take off in search of Dane without her.

He pushed the door open to the stairs and guided her behind him. "Stay back."

She nodded and they started down the stairs. Morgan didn't want to draw his firearm, but had no choice given the circumstances.

They got to the second floor and he opened the door, peered down the hall. Empty.

Halfway down to the first floor, he stopped at the sound of a whimper echoing up the stairs. Morgan put his finger to his lips and Julie shifted behind him. A few more steps and…

Morgan spotted the boy huddled on the bottom step. Dressed in his hospital gown, he clung to his clothes, his shoulders jerking as he fought back tears. Morgan holstered his gun and motioned Julie ahead.

"Dane?" she said.

He wiped at his eyes with the back of his hand and glanced up. "I didn't know where to go. You weren't here and…he called. He said Andy was dead and they were coming for me."

She sat next to him and put her arm around his shoulder. "Who called?"

"Henson. He said I should have come back, but I didn't so they killed Andy. It's my fault, he's dead because of me!"

"Shh, calm down."

"And now they're coming for me!"

Julie glanced at Morgan with worry in her eyes.

"How did he call you?" Morgan asked.

"On my cell."

"Where is it?"

Dane reached into his jeans bunched in his

lap and pulled out the phone. Morgan grabbed it. "We need to leave. Now."

"Morgan?" Julie questioned.

"We can't risk them tracking his GPS. We need to dump the phone and get back to Port Whisper."

"Do you want to get dressed?" she asked Dane.

"No time," Morgan said. "Come on, let's get to my truck."

He guided them down to the basement level and pushed open the door. Scanning the parking garage, he spotted a delivery van unloading supplies. Morgan handed Julie his keys.

"Get to the truck."

Morgan kept watch as Julie led Dane to the truck. Once they were safely inside, Morgan went to the delivery van and slipped Dane's phone under the front seat. He figured the van had other stops and would hopefully be headed in the opposite direction of Port Whisper.

Casting one last glance around the garage, and feeling confident they weren't being watched, he got into the truck and started it up.

"Dane, I need you to stay down. Can you do that for me?" he said.

"Yeah."

Dane disappeared from the rearview mirror. Calming his adrenaline rush, Morgan pulled out of the lot, keeping a keen eye out for vehicles that might be following them. A gray Chevy pulled out behind him. Actually, this could be a good thing, an opportunity to stop and challenge the driver and get some answers. If the guy was sent by Henson, this could be a solid lead.

Before pulling onto Highway 101 North, Morgan slowed down and signaled.

"What's wrong?" Julie asked.

"Someone's following us. I want to see what he does."

Instead of pulling over behind Morgan, the Chevy passed them. Morgan jotted the plate number on his dashboard notepad. He didn't want to sit on the side of the road any longer than necessary, so he handed Julie his phone. "Call Scott for me. Speed dial two."

She did and put the phone on speaker. "Hey, Chief."

"Scott, I need you to run a plate for me."

"Sure."

Julie read him the number.

"Get back to me as soon as possible," Morgan ordered.

"Yes, sir."

"How's everything in town?" Morgan asked.

"Waddingham's dog bit the Kingston kid and we had a fender bender on Front Street, but otherwise same as usual. Where are you?"

"On my way back. I'm bringing one of Julie's boys with us. We think he's involved in this case."

"Are we locking him up?"

Dane sat up, worried. Morgan eyed him in the rearview.

"No, he'll be a guest at Dad's house. Speaking of which, could you have a cruiser swing by the house every half hour or so, just until I get back?"

"Absolutely."

"Thanks—" Morgan paused "—Chief."

"Very funny. Get back here before the place falls apart."

"Check that. 'Bye."

Julie pressed the end button and placed the phone into the cup holder. "Do you think they've located your dad's house?"

"No, but it doesn't hurt to have a police presence cruise by."

Morgan glanced in his side-view mirror. "Dane, want to help me out?"

"It depends."

"Dane," Julie warned.

"Can you keep an eye out for cars that might be following us, especially a gray Chevy?" Morgan asked. "I'm going to pull off the highway before we get back to Port Whisper just to be sure, but I could use another set of eyes to keep watch."

"Sure, okay."

"And we'll stop by a Target to get you some clothes."

"What's wrong with my clothes?" Dane said.

"Thought you'd want something clean, but hey, if you want to wear those…"

"No, that's okay, I guess."

Julie glanced at him over the seat. "How about 'thanks, Morgan.'"

"Thanks," the kid grunted.

Morgan eyed Julie. "Keep an eye on your side-view mirror for me?"

She glanced at her mirror. "I don't like the sound of you calling Scott 'Chief.'"

"It's temporary."

She shot him a worried look. "I hope so. I would never forgive myself if I ruined your career."

"Do you ever forgive yourself for anything?"

She refocused on the mirror.

"Jules?"

"What?"

"I made the decision to step down, Lana made the decisions she did in high school that got her into trouble and Suzy made the choice to take the boat out at night."

"Don't."

"What, point out the fact that this whole beating-yourself-up thing is dangerously close to narcissism?"

"Morgan," she protested.

"Sorry, but it's a logical conclusion. You hold on to other people's angst and sorrow like you've created it for them. You didn't throw the street kids out of their homes, you didn't get them hooked on drugs. You—"

"That's enough," she said, her cheeks reddening.

"Why? What are you afraid of?"

"Everyone knowing the truth."

"Which is?"

"I'm a failure. I failed as a friend or Suzy would still be alive, I failed as a girlfriend and I failed as a counselor."

The car fell silent. She turned to look out her window and he regretted pushing her. She'd admitted to the demons chasing her, but to what end? Did speaking it out loud purge the fear from her system or just solidify it? He wished he didn't need to be so focused on avoiding their pursuers and keeping her safe.

He wished he could pull her into his arms and tell her that she was anything but a failure, that she was kind and smart and brave, for starters.

"Miss Burns?" Dane said from the backseat.

"Yes?"

"I just want you to know, I would have been dead by now if I hadn't met you."

The sight that greeted them when they pulled up to Morgan's house nearly took Julie's breath away. Mom had not only found the Christmas decorations, but had put them up in record time. Colorful lights trimmed the roofline of the house, spruce garland was wrapped around the porch railing and a fresh pine wreath with multicolored lights hung on the front door.

Morgan eyed the front door. "Now, I know they didn't find that in my garage."

"I don't want to know how Mom got the lights up on the roof. I don't like the thought of her on a ladder."

"I'm guessing Anderson helped out, or Scooner, or maybe even Sketch."

"You're not upset, are you?"

He parked in the back and glanced at her. "Why would I be upset?"

"I sensed you didn't want her finding the Christmas decorations."

"It's just been a long time since anything's been celebrated in Dad's house. I'm glad you and your family are changing that." He placed his hand over hers and her breath caught.

Suddenly Dane popped up in the backseat, awakening from a sound sleep. "Where are we?"

"My dad's house. Come on, let's get inside."

As they started up the back steps, the sound of Christmas music echoed through the window. Morgan opened the back door and the aroma that greeted them made Julie's mouth water.

She realized she hadn't eaten anything substantial in close to twenty-four hours and she was starving.

The table was set, the kettle was on and Mom greeted her with a kiss on the cheek. "I made your favorite, shepherd's pie." She glanced at Dane, who carried two shopping bags. "You'd better change, young man. We're expecting guests any minute now."

Just then, Lana pulled into the driveway.

Dane glanced frantically around as if looking for a place to hide. Or escape. Still dressed in his hospital gown beneath a jean jacket Morgan had bought him, the boy was obviously feeling exposed.

"Bathroom's upstairs on the right," Morgan said.

Dane rushed through the living room and up the stairs.

"The house looks great, Edith," Morgan said.

"Thanks. We took care of the outside today and tomorrow's goal is the living room. Are you getting a live tree this year, Morgan?"

"Hadn't given it much thought."

"I'll never forgot the time you and Julie went to Miller's Farm and cut down a seven-foot tree."

"That didn't fit in our living room." Julie smiled at the memory.

Morgan glanced out the kitchen window at Lana and Ashley, who approached the back steps carrying shopping bags from Tindle's Market.

"Is Sketch joining us?" Morgan asked.

"I'm sure he'll be here. Where Ashley goes, Sketch goes," Mom offered. She smiled and checked the pie. "Kind of reminds me of you two at their age."

For the first time since she'd been back, Julie didn't feel the need to scold Mom for bringing up their past. They had been close, in love, and it wasn't right to pretend it didn't happen.

Or that it wasn't happening again.

"I need water," Julie said, grabbing a glass and filling it with ice. She needed to do something to shock her back to reality. Perhaps she should dump a glass of ice water over her head?

Lana and Ashley came into the kitchen. "Wild rice was on sale, plus whole chickens and celery." She slid the bags onto the counter.

"You're making more food?" Julie asked.

"Chicken soup for tomorrow."

"You're spoiling me," Morgan said, stepping around Julie for a glass.

"It's my pleasure," Mom said. "Dinner will be ready in ten minutes."

"How can I help?" Julie said.

"No, no." Mom waved her off. "Sit, relax, tell us about our guest."

Suddenly, Sketch appeared in the doorway. "What guest?" His eyes caught Ashley's and she smiled. Sketch smiled back and glanced at the floor.

They were adorable. Morgan glanced at Julie and cracked his own smile. He must have been thinking the same thing.

"His name is Dane Simms," Julie said. "He's upstairs changing."

"Who is he?" Sketch flopped down at the kitchen table.

"One of the boys I counsel at Teen Life."

"Sounds like he got caught in the same net that snared Julie," Morgan added.

"Can he help solve the case?" Lana asked.

"Possibly," Morgan said.

"He needs to take it easy," Julie said. "We were at the hospital with him all night."

"Was he drugged out?" Sketch said.

"No." She glanced at Morgan. "He was dehydrated."

Sketch dumped his computer bag on the kitchen table.

"Nuh-uh," Mom said. "We're setting the table. Ashley, could you do the honors?"

"Sure."

"Sketch, I could use your help with something," Morgan said. "Come into the living room."

"Okay, Chief." He eyed Ashley. "Duty calls."

Sketch followed Morgan into the living room.

Ten minutes later, Edith was calling everyone to the table. Julie glanced toward the second floor.

"Do you want me to check on him?" Morgan asked.

"No, I'll do it." Julie went upstairs and found the bathroom door open, Dane's dirty clothes on the floor, but no Dane. Panic flooded her chest. "Dane?"

"In here."

She followed the sound of his voice into Morgan's room. Dane sat in the corner, freshly showered and dressed in the clothes Morgan had bought him, knees pulled to his chest. Julie sat on the bed a few inches from him.

"What's up, buddy?" she asked.

"I like this room."

She figured he would. "This was Morgan's room."

"He's got a lot of plaques and stuff."

"He had some good years in high school." She paused. "And some bad. Come on downstairs for dinner. You have to be starving."

Dane shrugged. "It sounds like there's a lotta people down there."

"Just family. Morgan, my mom, my sister, Lana, her assistant, Ashley, and Ashley's boyfriend, Sketch. He's seventeen. Like you."

"And he's probably a brain or jock or something."

"Actually, he's a high-school dropout. But yeah, he's kind of a computer brain. Come on." Julie stood and motioned for him to join her.

"I'll be down in a minute."

"I wouldn't wait too long. My mom's shepherd's pie is a favorite."

"I don't even know what that is."

"It's like hamburger meat, flavored with veggies and baked with mashed potatoes on top. She also made Jell-O salad, Christmas cookies and caramel-apple pie for dessert." She paused. "À la mode."

Dane absently licked his lips, but didn't move.

"Okay, well, I don't want to keep them waiting. See you in a few minutes." Julie headed downstairs, hoping she'd enticed him to join the family.

The family. A surge of contentment filled her

chest. Yes, this was a family, everyone gathering to celebrate a meal and their love for one another.

She breezed into the kitchen and sat next to Morgan.

"Is he joining us?" Morgan asked.

"He will, when he's ready." She glanced around the table. "He'll be skittish, so don't ask him a lot of questions. Offer as much unconditional love as possible."

Mom reached for Julie's and Lana's hands on either side of her. "A prayer," Mom said. "Lord, thank You for the blessing of family, friends and the bounty before us. Amen."

"Amen," everyone repeated.

Plates were passed to Mom and she dished out delicious shepherd's pie. Conversation centered around the fender bender in town, and whether the Waddinghams' dog should be locked up at the county pound for biting the Kingston kid.

"Tommy Kingston was probably asking for it," Sketch said.

"Why do you say that?" Morgan challenged.

"That kid is a menace. He rides his scooter like he's in the Indy 500, and teases the dog that lives behind them. It was about time a dog put him in his place."

"Sketch, that isn't nice," Mom said, then glanced up at the doorway. Julie guessed Dane had come down, but she knew he'd bolt if they made a big deal out of it.

"Mom," Julie said, hoping to distract her mother from saying something that would spook Dane, something as innocent as "we're happy to have you for dinner."

Edith glanced at Julie.

"Was there gravy to go along with the pie?" Julie asked.

"Oh, my land. Gravy." Mom popped up from her seat and poured gravy from a pot on the stove into a gravy boat. "Where is my head today?"

"Probably pickled from paint fumes," Morgan joked, following Julie's lead.

Ashley stared across the room at Dane.

"Ashley, how are the hotel-management classes going?" Julie asked.

Sketch must have nudged her under the table, because Ashley jerked her attention to Julie.

"Boring, beyond boring."

"She's stuck in geckers," Sketch said.

"What's a gecker?" Julie asked.

"General Education Course Curriculum Requirements, blah, blah," Sketch said.

"So, like—"

"Math, ugh." Ashley rolled her eyes. "Psychology, double ugh. History. Depressing."

"I don't know, I kinda liked history," Lana offered.

As the conversation continued, Julie shifted closer to Morgan to make room for Dane. Sure, Dane would be sitting next to her mom, and perhaps that terrified him considering his mother abused him, forcing him to run away, but he had to sense the goodness of Julie's mom.

Mom passed the gravy. "My favorite class was literature. The classics—Brontë, Hemingway, Jane Austen."

Sketch made quotation marks with his fingers. "Love stories."

"Not all of them," Morgan piped up. "Hemingway wrote *The Old Man and the Sea*. Not exactly a romance."

"I think the dude was secretly in love with the marlin."

The table burst out laughing as Mom grabbed Dane's plate and scooped a healthy portion of pie. She placed it in front of him and asked, "Gravy?"

He nodded, but didn't speak. At least he hadn't rushed out of the room.

As Mom poured gravy onto his pie, Julie continued the conversation about Ashley's classes, and Lana contributed by saying she hoped Ashley could earn extra credit by working at Stone Soup.

"She's getting a hotel-restaurant management degree, so I'd think they'd credit her for all the time she's spent helping me with the business," Lana said.

"I worked at a pizza place," Dane offered, eyes focused on his meal.

"The best pizza in Seattle," Julie added.

Morgan put his fork down and reached for his phone. He eyed the caller ID. "Excuse me." He went into the living room and took the call.

"What's your favorite?" Sketch asked Dane.

Dane glanced at him in question.

"Pizza?"

"Hawaiian. Ham and pineapple."

"Now there's an interesting combination," Mom said.

Dane took a hearty bite of shepherd's pie, then another, and a third.

"Don't forget to leave room for dessert," Mom said with a smile. "We have apple pie and Christmas cookies."

Morgan returned, worry creasing his forehead.

"Morgan?" Julie questioned.

"That was Scott." He glanced past Julie to Mom. "Apparently someone broke into your house."

# *Chapter Fifteen*

"I knew they'd find me. It's my fault," Dane said.

"None of this is your fault," Julie said, placing a hand on his shoulder. "Don't talk that way."

"It could be a coincidence," Morgan offered. "At any rate, I'm headed over there to check things out."

Julie stood. "I'm coming with you."

Morgan touched her shoulder. "No, you're staying here, where it's safe. Sketch, Dane, I'm relying on you to watch over the ladies. Can you do that?"

"Absolutely," Sketch said.

Dane nodded. "Yeah."

"Good." Morgan gave Julie a hug. "I'll be back as soon as I can."

As he walked out the back door, Julie gathered her strength and knew it was up to her to keep the faith and stay positive. She would not let these bullies terrorize her or her family any longer, and she wouldn't be punished for getting into a line of work that she knew in her heart was a worthy cause. As Dane had said in the car, he would have been dead by now if he hadn't met Julie.

Taking a deep breath, Julie turned to face the group at the table. "Who's ready for dessert?"

"I'll clear," Lana offered, picking up on Julie's cue.

"I'll cut the pie," Mom said. "Dane, take your time and finish your dinner. We'll make sure there's dessert for you."

"What can I do?" Ashley asked.

"Actually, I'm going to get my files," Julie said. "Sketch, I want you to go through them and see if any red flags pop up."

"Yes, ma'am."

Julie went upstairs and grabbed her files. Even though the threat felt closer than ever, a renewed sense of determination flooded her body. She'd said she wasn't going to be afraid anymore, that she wasn't going to let them terrorize her. Yet she was still running from her stalker, hiding out and waiting for the attack.

No more.

As she came downstairs, Dane was waiting for her.

"Hey, what's wrong?" she asked.

"The chief asked me to watch out for you, so I am."

"Thanks, but perhaps Sketch could use your help."

She led him back into the kitchen.

"What can I do?" Dane asked.

"Tell him everything you know about Henson, when you met and where, what kind of car he drives, what he looks like. Give Sketch specifics about Andy, things he told you that might help us figure out who Henson is working for."

"Whoa, you're sounding like the chief," Sketch joked.

"Thanks," Julie said. "I'm going to make a timeline of everything that's happened since Andy disappeared and you were kidnapped. If we put everything out there, Sketch might be able to make some connections."

"If there's anything to connect, I'll figure it out," Sketch said.

Dane sat across from Sketch, and Sketch fired off questions. Julie pulled out a pad of paper and wrote everything down, while Lana and Mom made tea and coffee, sliced pie and served it to the group.

Julie realized that although she was taking the offense, she was also distracting herself from what Morgan was doing. She worried that whoever had broken into Mom's house might have done so to flush Julie out of hiding. They could be waiting for Morgan, hiding out in the bushes or behind the garage.

She stopped her head from spinning in that direction. Morgan was a professional; he knew how to handle potentially dangerous situations. And his deputy chief was on-site, so no one would risk attacking two cops. Would they?

She had to believe Morgan and Scott would be okay. Mom slid the apple pie in front of Julie. "I'm very proud of you," Mom said.

"What? Why?"

"For being strong and not blaming yourself."

"Don't be too proud. I was running away, re-member? That's how I ended up back in Port Whisper."

"Sweetie, I think something else brought you back. You let your heart lead you back where you'd be safe and grounded, where you could deal with your challenge with the support of family and friends." Mom shifted next to her, cradling a cup of tea. "Look at you now, my little detective."

"I don't know about little," Lana joked.

"Leave it to my little sister not to let me get a big head."

"What other companies or donors do you work with at Teen Life?" Sketch asked.

Julie rattled off a few companies that generously donated time or money. "Why do you ask?"

"The chief asked me to do a comprehensive search of anyone affiliated with your place. What about this Helen lady?"

"She's harmless. Resentful, but harmless."

"And some guy named William?"

"What are you doing, going down our staff list?"

"Yep."

"William did a few years in the private sector and didn't feel like he was having the impact he wanted, so he joined our team.

"Speaking of William, I need to check on him." She pulled out her cell.

"Check this out," Sketch said to Dane, who looked over his shoulder. "I can find out the history of the five major companies that donate to Teen Life, who owns them, how many employees they have, if they've turned a profit in the last five years."

Julie called William's cell number. It rang four times before he picked up. "This is William."

"It's Julie. How are you?"

"Better, although I look like I went five rounds with George Foreman."

"I'm so sorry."

"I'm not. I needed the time off. How are things on your end?"

"Okay. Dane found us. He was terrified, William. Someone's been testing drugs on these kids."

"What! Who?"

"I have no idea. We're still trying to piece that together."

"I hope you do it quick."

"Me, too." She considered his comment. "William? What's going on at work?"

"Everything's fine."

"Try again."

"I didn't want to worry you, what with everything you have going on."

"I can handle it."

"Dynacorp is determined to have a meeting tomorrow and Helen doesn't think she's ready. I don't think it's a good idea for me to walk in looking like I was hit by a truck, and Andrea's mother is sick, so she's distracted. There's no one to present tomorrow. I'm afraid…"

"We're going to lose their funding?"

Dynacorp was Teen Life's biggest donor. She hated to consider what would happen if they pulled their support.

"Maybe I'll call them, explain the situation," she said.

"What will you say?"

"Good question. Wish I had an answer."

"How's Dane?"

She glanced across the room at Dane and Sketch, who seemed to be getting along just fine. "Better than last night. He was dehydrated, and they found an odd substance in his bloodstream."

"Do they know what it was?"

"They're not sure."

"May I speak with Dane?"

"Sure." She handed Dane the phone.

"William wants to say hi."

"Hello?" Dane got up and wandered into the living room.

Julie went to help Mom and Lana finish the dinner dishes, but Mom's hip bumped her out of the way. "You relax," Mom said.

"Mom, you're spoiling me."

"It's about time someone did. Go on, help Sketch do that computer stuff."

Julie sat beside Sketch and eyed the computer. A few minutes later Dane came into the kitchen and handed Julie the phone.

"Wait, did William—"

"He had to go," Dane said, not making eye contact.

Julie sensed he was still blaming himself for Andy's death. She wanted to say something to help him release his angst, but Julie knew better than anyone that the only person who would give Dane peace was Dane himself.

Wasn't that what Julie had learned this past week? That it was about time she forgave herself?

She considered that there was an upside to this disastrous week. It forced her to face her own dark places, her guilt over things she truly had no control over.

A sense of peace eased into her heart and she closed her eyes. She liked the feeling and opened her heart to God. *Thank You, Lord, for showing me the way. And thank You for bringing Morgan back into my life.*

When this was all over, and she hoped it would be soon, Julie would have a heart-to-heart with Morgan. She'd thank him for showing her the path of forgiveness, for being so patient with her and being her rock through all this.

"Hey, you asleep?" Sketch teased.

Julie opened her eyes. "Just thinking."

"Well, think about this." He pointed to his computer screen. "Two deposits were made into Helen's account over the last six months. Five grand each."

"Wow, where'd that come from?" Julie said.

"It was cash, so there's no way to trace it. But the government's going to be all over her for that."

Dane leaned against the kitchen counter, eating his pie.

"Dane, you can sit down," Julie encouraged.

Dane swallowed his last bite of pie and handed the plate to Julie's mom. "I'm gonna go lie down."

"Take Morgan's room," Julie said.

"Okay." Dane wandered out of the kitchen and went upstairs.

"Is he going to be okay?" Lana asked.

"We'll make sure he is."

They spent the next three hours poring over documentation about Teen Life's five major donors. Nothing odd or suspicious popped up. The strangest thing was Helen's deposits.

Morgan called to let Julie know he'd be home soon, that he was checking out a lead about the break-in. Lana gave Ashley and Sketch a ride home. Edith finished wiping down the kitchen counter and had gone upstairs.

But Julie couldn't relax until Morgan came home. She read a book in the kitchen, getting up every twenty minutes or so to glance out the window. Where was he?

She turned around and spotted Dane in the doorway.

"Whoa," she said, "you startled me."

"I'm sorry," Dane said.

"Stop, you have nothing to be sorry about."

Dane walked into the kitchen and pulled a knife from the butcher block.

"You hungry again?" she said.

He turned and pointed the knife at her.

"Dane?"

"Give me your necklace."

She automatically touched the locket Andy had given her. "What? Why?"

"I need it!" he shouted.

"Shh," she put out her hand. She didn't want him waking Mom and terrifying her.

"What's this about? Talk to me."

"Just give it to me," he cried, his eyes tearing.

He didn't want to be doing this, but something compelled him to threaten Julie with a knife.

"Give it or I'll take it from you."

But he didn't take a step toward her. He was frozen in place, hoping that she'd give him what he'd asked for.

"Why do you need it?"

"Does it matter?"

"It does to me."

"I need it to buy drugs."

She knew it was a lie, she could read it in his green eyes.

"I don't believe you."

"Don't make me hurt you!"

"I don't believe you will."

"Why won't you just give it to me?" he challenged.

"Because you're not a thief or a drug addict. You're a good kid who's in a bad place." She extended her hand. "Let me help you out."

"You can't!"

Oddly enough, she didn't feel as if she was in real danger. Was she being unrealistic? No, she had faith in Dane, faith that he was a good kid who'd been forced into a corner. But by whom?

"You called and asked for our help, Dane. Let me help you now."

"I was playing you. I'm working for Henson."

Another lie, but calling him out on it would only escalate the tension in the room.

"I'm sorry to hear that," she said.

A tear escaped his right eye and trailed down his cheek. "This is your last chance. Give me the necklace!"

"You're going to have to take it from me."

He took a step forward, but she didn't waver.

"I'm...sorry," he croaked.

"I know. And I believe in you, Dane."

"You shouldn't!" He tossed the knife onto the kitchen table and raced out the back door. Julie automatically went after him, but having lived on the streets, he was fast and clever. She stood on the back porch, looking through the neighbor's yard.

Dane was gone. And terrified.

Another piece of the puzzle. After all, the necklace wasn't anything special, probably worth no more than twenty bucks.

Just then, a squad car pulled into the driveway. Morgan. How would she explain this situation to him? He'd want to arrest Dane for sure, and she didn't want the boy to have another mark on his record.

As she went to greet the driver, she realized it wasn't Morgan, but rather Deputy Chief Finnegan behind the wheel. Panic shuddered down her spine.

He got out of the car, wearing a concerned frown. "Where is Morgan?" Julie said.

"The chief wanted me to tell you he's okay."

"What happened?" She gripped the railing for support.

"He was following a suspicious car and was run off the road."

# Chapter Sixteen

The world tipped sideways as Julie struggled to stay calm and grounded.

"Take me to him," she ordered, walking to the cruiser.

"He wants you to stay here. It's obvious they're in Port Whisper. He thinks you'll be safer at home."

"I'll be safe with Morgan." She got into the cruiser and waited.

Scott slid in behind the wheel and started up the car.

"Where is he, exactly?" she said.

"Doc Saunders's office."

"How badly is he hurt?"

"He's got a cut across his forehead and he's a little banged up, but otherwise okay."

Okay, but run off the road. She fought back the image of Morgan stuck in a car while the bad guys drove off, or worse, approached the car to finish what they'd started.

The nightmare flashed across her mind. A gunshot. Morgan falling to his knees.

Dead.

Dread shot through her body at the thought of a world without Morgan, and that's when she realized how much she still loved him. Not just the boy she'd watched sunrises with, but the honorable man he'd become. A man who'd opened her heart to God after it had been closed for so many years.

She couldn't think about that now. She had to figure out a way to end this and keep Morgan safe from the mysterious Henson and whoever he worked for.

"Did they take X-rays?" she asked.

"Doc didn't think it was necessary. I'm sure he'll be okay. He's a tough guy."

Tough and tender. Yep, that was Morgan. In her eyes, he was perfect and he deserved a good life. She didn't want him giving up his career in Port Whisper for her, and although her job had grown dangerous, the street kids needed her.

*I would have been dead by now if I hadn't met you.*

Dane's words. New worry whipped through her about where Dane was and why he'd wanted her necklace. Should she even tell Morgan? No, he needed to rest, to recover from his accident.

They pulled up to Doc Saunders's office and she nearly jumped from the car before Scott put the cruiser in Park.

"Hang on," he called after her, but she was already banging on the office door.

Doc Saunders opened the door and let her in. "Julie. Good to see you."

"How's Morgan?"

Morgan stepped out from an examining room and she steeled herself against the sight of the bandage across his forehead, and the way he clutched his arm to his midsection.

Scott walked in behind her.

"I told you to keep her at the house," Morgan said in an angry tone.

"I tried," Scott answered.

"I wanted to make sure you were okay."

"I'm fine."

Tension stretched between them.

"Why don't you two talk in the examining room?" Doc Saunders suggested.

Morgan went back into the room. Julie followed and shut the door. "I'm so sorry."

"Stop, I don't need your pity."

"I think it's called sympathy."

"I don't need that, either." Morgan sat in a chair, not on the examining table, and winced.

"What can I do for you?" she said.

"Go back to the house where it's safe."

"I'm not leaving your side until—"

"Until what? This case is solved? We're no closer to having answers than we were a week ago. You said it yourself. Face it, Jules, I'm not a good enough detective to get ahead of this thing. You're better off going back to Seattle."

"You've kept me safe for a whole week. Who knows what would have happened if I'd stayed there."

He pinned her with blue-green eyes. "You would have contacted Ethan and he could have helped you. Instead, you come back here and we're all chasing our tails like a pack of dogs."

"Not true. Sketch flagged some questionable activity for—"

"Sketch. He's a kid. Even a kid can do better than me."

His words were laced with insecurity and doubt, his tone sounding much like that of an eighteen-year-old.

"What are you really upset about here, Morgan?"

"My own incompetence."

She kneeled beside him and touched his thigh. "Is it incompetent to keep me and my mom safe? To keep your town running and

chase down leads? You've done everything possible to solve this case."

"But it's not enough." He pinned her again
with his intense eyes. "Face it, Jules, I'm not
enough."

"Morgan, don't—"

"Stop." He stood and opened the door, went
out into the main office and left her behind.

"Am I good to go?" she heard him ask the
doctor.

Julie shifted onto the chair where Morgan
had just been sitting and realization struck: he
thought he'd failed her. From now on, whenever he looked into her eyes, he'd see his own
failure there.

She couldn't stand the thought of being a
source of pain and self-loathing for Morgan.
She needed to do the right thing.

And let him go.

As Scott drove them back to Dad's house.
Morgan could hardly look at Julie, he was so
ashamed that he'd failed her once again. But
what had he expected? As she'd pointed out, he
was a small-town cop in a community where
the biggest crime was petty vandalism.

Morgan couldn't believe the perps got the
jump on him, but then he wasn't expecting a
rear assault. He'd had the suspicious Ford in his

sights when someone had slammed him from behind. Hard.

At least he'd called in the Ford's plate number before the collision. One good move on Morgan's part.

Scott dropped them off at Dad's house. "Thanks, Scott."

"Sure thing. I'll call you when I get registration information on the Ford."

He escorted Julie up the back steps and into the living room. Morgan flopped down on the couch.

"I'm glad Mom's asleep." She glanced upstairs. "By the way, Dane left."

"Left? Where did he go?"

"I don't know. He—" she hesitated "—just left."

She was leaving something out, he could tell. "What aren't you telling me?"

"He tried to steal my locket."

"What? Why?"

"I have no idea. He said he needed to sell it for drug money, but he didn't demand my wallet or Mom's. He was terrified, Morgan."

Morgan sat up. "I should—"

"No." She put her hands out. "Just let it go for tonight, okay?"

He flopped back against the couch. "You still believe in that kid, don't you?"

"Yep. There are some things you just know... in your gut."

Like how Morgan would never get this woman out of his system. Who was he kidding?

"Will you be okay?" she asked.

"Sure, the doc gave me pain meds. Should sleep like a baby."

"I've been thinking, maybe it's best if I head back to Seattle tomorrow."

It felt as if someone had swung a baseball bat at his already bruised ribs. Sure, he'd been the one to suggest it an hour ago, but that was out of frustration.

"If you think that's best," he said, not looking at her.

"Do you?"

He glanced up, into her golden eyes, wanting to ask her to stay, to make a life with him. That would be selfish on his part.

"Considering we haven't made any progress since you've been here? Yeah, I guess you'd be better off working with more experienced professionals. Get help from Ethan, or hire yourself a private investigator. E might know someone."

Her gaze drifted down to the floor and she fingered the stair railing.

"Okay, well, sweet dreams." She raced up the stairs, away from him.

Out of his life. Again.

\* \* \*

Tossing and turning for hours, Julie glanced at the bedside clock. Four a.m. She couldn't sleep, couldn't stop thinking about Morgan.

He was letting her go. He thought it best if she left, which meant his feelings for her weren't strong enough to keep her in Port Whisper, and he'd accepted the fact that she'd been selfish by bringing her troubles to the small town.

It would be hard to leave again, more like heartbreaking. Between falling for Morgan and relishing the warmth, the love of being around family and friends, she dreaded going back to her solitary life. But it was the right thing to do.

Her cell phone vibrated and she eyed the caller ID. She recognized William's number.

"William?"

"No, but how about a trade? His life for your files?"

She jackknifed in bed. "Who is this?"

"The name's Henson."

"Let me speak with him." She gripped the phone.

"Julie?"

"William, are you—"

"Aren't you tired of this game?" Henson said. "Being followed, threatened? Watching loved ones get hurt…because of you?"

"Let him go."

"When I get your files. Meet us at six a.m., Timberlake Lighthouse."

"It's too isolated. I'll meet you at Squamish Harbor, north dock, at seven."

"You really think you're in a position to negotiate?"

"Do you want the files or not?" She didn't know where her sudden strength came from, but she embraced it. She'd been in enough negotiations to know if she gave everything up at the beginning, she'd come out the loser.

And probably end up dead.

"Seven at Squamish Harbor," he confirmed. "Don't tell anyone where you're going or my associate will finish the job he started on your cop boyfriend."

The line went dead.

Heart racing, she got dressed and fought back the panic in her gut. She considered telling someone. Morgan, or Scott? No, Henson demanded she come alone. An image flashed across her mind: Henson strangling William in front of her because she didn't follow his orders.

She'd put everyone at risk by involving them in the first place. She needed to stop hiding behind family and friends.

And end this thing.

She grabbed her fleece and backpack and headed downstairs, strategizing ways to get

through this safe and unharmed. She'd nego-
tiated a better meeting spot. That was a good
start. Squamish Harbor, about an hour away,
was relatively busy at seven in the morning with
early risers headed out on their boats. Just in
case Henson changed his mind about doing her
harm, she made sure she had her pepper spray.

As she stepped onto the first floor, she froze
at the sight of Morgan, fast asleep, his arm
protectively stretched across bruised ribs. He
looked peaceful and fragile, and she ached to
walk over and spread the blanket across his
body. She couldn't risk it. It would be too tempt-
ing to kiss him one last time.

"I love you, Morgan," she whispered. Even if
he was asleep, she wanted those three words to
be the last thing she said to him. After all, there
was always the chance she wasn't going to come
out of this alive. She shook off the thought and
headed into the kitchen where she found Mom's
car keys in a ceramic bowl.

In case attempting to save William was the
last thing she did on this earth...

She pulled a piece of scrap paper from a top
drawer and wrote the words down just in case
they didn't register in Morgan's subconscious.
She folded the paper and wrote his name across it.

No matter what happened next, he needed to
know that she loved him.

She pulled the door closed and touched the glass, imagining Morgan, Mom, Lana, Ashley and Sketch seated around the dinner table, laughing, joking. With a deep breath, she turned and headed for Mom's car. She was doing this for them. Her family.

*God, please keep them safe.*

Morgan awakened with a start, glancing around the room to get his bearings.

*I love you, Morgan.*

Julie's voice. Great, now he was dreaming about her. Of course he was, by this time tomorrow she'd be nothing but a dream, a distant memory.

That would tear him apart for months to come.

He sat up and groaned. Fighting back the pain of bruised ribs, he went into the kitchen for a glass of water. He flipped on the light and spotted a note on the counter. Julie's handwriting. He couldn't bring himself to open it, so he shoved it into his jacket pocket.

He placed his glass in the sink and headed back to the couch. If only he could stop thinking about her and get a few more hours of sleep.

Closing his eyes, her tender smile filled his mind.

*Thump, thump.*

Morgan sat up, waited, trying to determine where the sound was coming from.

*Thump, thump, thump.* The back porch.

He pulled his firearm out of its holster and crept through the living room. He poked his head around the corner, but didn't see anyone on the other side of the door.

*Thump, thump.*

He whipped the door open and spotted Dane sprawled on his back, pounding on the porch with a closed fist.

"Dane?" Morgan shoved the gun into the back of his jeans and kneeled beside him. "What happened?"

"Miss Burns...you've got to stop her. It's a trap."

"Come on." Morgan pulled Dane to his feet and noticed a bloodstain on his shirt.

"Who did this?"

"Henson," he said, gasping for breath.

Morgan pulled out a dish towel and ran it under water. "Where are you hurt?"

"Forget about me." He gripped Morgan's hand as he tried to get a look at his wound. "You've got to stop her."

"She's fine, she's..." Then Morgan remembered her note. He dropped the dish towel and raced up the stairs, adrenaline numbing his aches and pains.

He whipped open her door...

The bed was empty.

"Morgan?" Edith said, wandering into the hallway. "What's all the ruckus?"

"Get dressed. I'm taking you to Caroline's."

"Where's Julie?"

"In trouble. We've gotta go."

Morgan pulled out his phone and called his deputy chief. "Scotty, sorry to wake you. We've got a situation. Julie's gone and Dane says it's a trap. Meet me at the station."

"Yes, sir."

Morgan glanced at Julie's mom, whose face paled with worry.

"I'm gonna get her back," Morgan assured.

And this time he was never letting her go.

# Chapter Seventeen

Julie clung to her files and got out of the car, dread knotting her shoulder muscles. Feeling for the pepper spray in her pocket, she glanced to her left, where she could see the Squamish Police Department—she remembered it from the time she and Morgan were questioned for being on the pier early in the morning. They'd gone out to watch the sunrise and had fallen asleep, being discovered by a patrolman starting his day shift.

At 7:00 a.m. That's why she picked this place. And this time.

She focused ahead and spotted two men standing at the end of the pier. Exposed, just as she'd planned. She felt safer being out in the open. As she walked down the pier, the planked wood creaked under her tennis shoes. She focused on William, the primary reason she was putting herself at risk.

It was the longest walk of her life, but it would be over soon. She'd toss the files at Henson and leave with William. In a perfect world.

Henson was short and stocky, wearing a baseball cap pulled low over his eyes, and a leather jacket. William wore an overcoat, his arms behind his back. Henderson held on to one of them.

She stopped fifty feet away.

"Let William go," she ordered.

"The files?"

She waved them.

"Toss them and I'll let him go."

She took a few more steps and dropped them onto the wood planks. Henson motioned for William to walk to Julie. A sinking feeling settled low. This felt too easy.

She noticed a speedboat at the end of the dock. Henson had his getaway figured out. Now if she could only dream up an escape route for herself and William.

William approached her and Julie studied his face. He didn't make eye contact, worrying her. What had Henson done to him?

"William, I'm so sorry." She reached out and touched his arm.

"Me, too." He grabbed her locket and yanked it off her neck. She stumbled back.

"What are you—"

Henson raced across the dock and grabbed her arm, dragging her toward the boat.

"William!"

He flanked her other side. "If you'd just given Dane the locket…"

"Why do you need the locket?"

"Get her into the boat," Henson said.

"Henson!" a man called from behind them.

They spun around. Morgan stood at the other end of the pier, exposed, pointing his firearm at them.

"Put the gun down," Henson threatened, pressing the barrel of his gun to Julie's temple.

Clenching his jaw, Morgan slowly lowered his firearm.

"Morgan, no!"

A shot rang out as William flung Julie into the boat and jumped in next to her.

Morgan had figured it out, he'd come for her.

Henson sped away. The thought of him shooting Morgan arced panic through her chest. Julie realized the farther from land they went, the bigger the chance they were going to shoot her and dump her body. She whipped out the pepper spray and shot at William's eyes. He jumped up.

"Ahhh!"

Henson glanced over his shoulder. "What the—"

Julie fired at Henson, but he deflected the spray. She shoved a blinded William into Henson's back and dived into the frigid water. Shock flooded her body as she struggled against the weight of her clothes.

She was an excellent swimmer, but in these cold waters she had about a minute before her limbs grew numb, even with two layers of clothes.

A muffled shot rang out. Were they shooting at her? She couldn't think about that. She had to get back to the pier.

Back to Morgan.

She fought back the panic swallowing her as surely as the frigid harbor waters. She wasn't ready to leave this earth yet. She had more teenagers to help—to save.

*I'm not done, Lord.*

Fighting the cold and her tightening muscles, she stroked the best she could. *One, two, three.*

*Keep going,* she coached herself. But her clothes were dragging her down and her arms felt as if they were cutting through cement.

*One, two...*

Her arms cramped. She could barely reach out. She took a deep breath and let go. Drifted. Floated. Gunfire echoed across the water. She couldn't tell if she'd been shot, her skin ice-cold, numb.

The water swallowed her, pulling her down, down…

This must be how Suzy had felt just before she'd died. Julie struggled against her own surrender. As she searched for hope, her mind flooded with despair.

Suddenly someone grabbed her, pulling her up, breaking through the water's surface.

"I got you, Jules."

She looked up at the bright morning sky. Then a voice said, "Stay with me. Don't you dare give up."

Morgan.

She closed her eyes and drank in the sound of his voice. Her love. The man who owned a part of her heart.

And she fell unconscious.

The past few hours had been a blur, Julie realized as she sat on Morgan's couch being tended by her mom, Lana and Morgan. Mom kept adjusting her blankets, adding more, tucking them in just so. Lana rubbed Julie's leg, and Morgan brought her a cup of hot tea.

"I'm okay, really," Julie said. The fact that she didn't remember what had happened after Morgan rescued her bothered her a bit.

"The doctor said to rest and drink plenty of fluids," her mom said.

"You know what I could use?" Julie said.

The three of them waited.

"Chocolate-chip-bacon cookies."

Mom smiled and stood. "Coming right up. Lana, come help me."

They went into the kitchen and Morgan sat on the coffee table. "Green mango, your favorite." He offered her the tea.

"Thanks." She took it, their hands touching.

She wanted to put the tea down and hold his hand, soak up his warmth, but he pulled away a little too quickly.

"So fill me in," she said.

"Where do I start?" he sighed.

*By telling me you love me?*

"Dynacorp was behind this whole thing. Apparently Andy put the drug powder into the locket he gave you, which was proof they were into something illegal."

"Which was what, exactly?"

"The drug they were trying out is a synthetic meant to get you high. It's very expensive, marketed to white-collar professionals. But they had to test it out first to determine the side effects. Who better to test it on than street kids who wouldn't be missed if they died?"

"Dane tried to steal it from me."

"Because Henson said to get the locket and bring it to him or he'd kill you."

"What about my files?"

"They needed to destroy evidence of any kids involved in the testing. Those kids happened to be in your caseload."

"So this whole time they wanted my files *and* my locket?"

"Yep. Ethan and the DEA are making their case. Henson was arrested." He paused. "As was William."

"I can't believe he was involved."

"It was a big payoff for a guy making forty grand a year. He'd feed kids to Henson for testing. When Andy called from William's office, William was using him to expose your location. And the other night when William spoke with Dane on the phone?"

She nodded.

"He told Dane to get the locket. That's why Dane threatened you."

"But he couldn't hurt me."

"No, he's a good kid. There might be a spot for him at Horizon Farms once that gets off the ground."

"That would be amazing."

"Yes, it would."

"What about Helen and the mysterious deposits in her bank account?"

"A gift from an elderly aunt who passed away. She only kept cash."

"Oh."

A moment of silence passed between them. Julie wished she could get into Morgan's head and know what he was thinking.

"Now I have a question for you," Morgan said.

"Sure."

"Why didn't you ask for my help when you got the call from Henson?"

"Because he threatened to kill you if I didn't come alone."

"You were trying to protect me?"

"Yes, of course."

"You sure it's not something else?"

"Like what?"

"That you didn't think I could protect you?"

"Morgan—"

"It's okay, Jules, I get it. I'm just a small-town cop."

And not good enough for Jules. She knew that was his secret fear, even when they'd dated. Shame colored his eyes and she hated that she put it there.

She knew every time he looked at her he'd see his own failure, even though he'd saved her life.

She loved Morgan with all her heart, but

couldn't bear to see the pain in his eyes, his self-perceived failure.

"What's next on your agenda?" he said. "Now that you're safe?"

"Haven't given it much thought. I guess I should probably return to Seattle."

"The kids need you."

"Yes."

He nodded, glancing into the coffee cup he clutched between his hands. "Well, you know what's best."

*Leaving me,* she heard. How many times would she hurt this man? She had to do the right thing and walk away, for good this time. Release him into the arms of a sweet woman like Anna.

"What will you do?" she said.

"Finish up the house, sell it."

But that's not what she was asking.

"How's your dad?"

"As well as can be expected. They're moving him to a facility where he'll get twenty-four-hour care. He wants me to sell the house to help pay for it."

"And your job as police chief?"

"I need to think about that."

Her heart sank. He was an amazing chief, but was questioning his own abilities because of her.

"You belong here," she said.

"And you don't, I know. We don't have to go through this again."

"That's not what I meant."

Mom breezed into the room and brought Julie the phone. "You've got a call."

"Could you take a message?" she said, not taking her eyes off Morgan.

"I'd better check in." He leaned forward and kissed her on the forehead. "Be well."

Morgan turned his back on Julie and left. She stared at the spot where he'd just been sitting, regret tearing through her.

"Honey?" Mom said, offering the phone.

Julie took it. "Hello?"

"Julie, it's Joe, with Horizon Farms. How are you feeling?"

"Tired." *Devastated.*

"Well, before you head back to Seattle, I was wondering if you'd have time to talk about the farm. I could use some more advice."

"Sure, can I call you tomorrow?"

"Absolutely."

"Thanks."

She handed Mom the phone and leaned against the pillows. It probably wasn't a bad idea to distract herself by helping others. At least she'd feel competent at one thing, because she surely felt incompetent at love.

"Sweetie—" Mom shifted onto the coffee table "—what's happening between you and Morgan?"

"Nothing."

"But he loves you so."

"And I love him. Which is why I have to leave."

# Chapter Eighteen

A week later Morgan sat across from Sketch at the Turnstyle, going over Sketch's business plan. The community had rallied behind Morgan to step back into the chief role, but he was taking his time, needing to reevaluate his life, his future.

Reevaluate? More like spin in circles. Without Julie in his life, he felt anything but grounded. He fought the darkness, the grief of losing the woman he loved. But she'd chosen to leave again, and he couldn't blame her, not when he'd let her down. He could see it in her eyes.

"You're an idiot."

Morgan glanced up at Sketch. "What did you say?"

"You heard me."

"I could arrest you for that."

"You're not chief, remember?"

"I'm still an officer of the law."

"And an idiot."

"Where's this coming from?"

"Fool me once, shame on you. Fool me twice, shame on me. That's you."

"Still not getting it."

"You let her go again? What's wrong with you?"

"She chose to leave."

"Ashley says because she loves you too much."

"That makes no sense."

"No? Lana told her that Julie left because she thought it was best for you, that she's bad for you."

"She left because she knew I wasn't good enough." Morgan couldn't believe he'd uttered the words to a teenager.

"An idiot narcissist." Sketch shook his head and tapped at his keyboard.

"Look, I love her, but I don't want to keep her someplace where she's not happy. So I let her go."

"Great, yeah, you love her so much you let her go. She loves you so much she left. You guys are the definition of dysfunctional."

"What makes you so smart about relationships?"

Sketch pinned him with intense blue eyes. "I

watch people. A lot. I've also been taking psych classes online. You want my opinion?"

"Not particularly."

"Tough."

"I can see why you got kicked out of school."

Sketch ignored the immature comment. "You're making this all about you—'Julie doesn't have faith in me, I couldn't protect her, she's better than me.' Get over yourself. You kept her safe in your dad's house for a week, saved her from drowning and got her interested in God again."

"What?"

"That's what Lana said, that Julie's talking about going to church. What I don't get is why you're so dense. She loves you, you love her. What's the problem?"

"It's more complicated than that."

"No, it really isn't. And love isn't something you just throw away because it's hard."

"Kid, I appreciate the counseling session, but I'm a bit older than you and have a little more life experience about these things."

Sketch got out of the booth and grabbed his laptop. "That's right, put me down 'cause I'm a kid. Great defense mechanism." He started to walk away.

"Hey, I didn't mean—"

Sketch turned to him. "Love is a gift, dude.

You keep throwing it away like a used paper towel because your ego can't take the hit, or you're scared, I dunno. When are you gonna grow up and stop being a coward?"

Sketch stormed out of the restaurant, leaving Morgan speechless. He'd planned to fight for Julie this time, but hadn't had it in him after seeing the look of pity in her eyes. Or had it been something else?

He reached into his pocket for spare bills to cover his and Sketch's coffees. Instead, he pulled out a folded piece of paper. Julie's note.

He was tempted to toss it into the trash on his way out.

*When are you going to grow up and stop being a coward?*

Was the kid right? Was Morgan still clinging to the past? He'd accused Julie of running, but wasn't that exactly what he was doing? Running from himself? From their love?

He slowly opened the note and read:

*Morgan, please know I love you with all my heart. Always have. Always will.*
*Love, Julie*

He folded it and glanced out the window, wondering how he could have been so blind. To his own faults, to Julie's love. He'd accused her of taking responsibility for everyone else's decisions, yet he was giving up on their love because he was afraid he wasn't good enough?

"You're right, kid," he muttered. "Time to grow up."

He left the restaurant and went to find Lana. He needed help, and fast.

One good thing Julie had learned from the tumultuous week in Port Whisper was to take care of herself. Morgan had pointed out that she hadn't taken a vacation in years. No time like the present.

She pulled into a parking spot at Friday Harbor and sighed. Lana had convinced her to start her getaway with a tour of the San Juan Islands. She'd even made the reservation on a friend's boat.

Julie had booked a few nights in a cozy bed-and-breakfast where she could relax. The Inn was primed for the holidays with fresh evergreen swags stretched across the fireplace mantel, white lights and gold ornaments decorating a Christmas tree in the corner of the living room, and the aroma of hot cider filling the house. Julie struggled to embrace the Christmas spirit, but her heavy heart fought back her joy.

After her weekend in Friday Harbor, she was

thinking about visiting a warm climate. She was making up for lost time.

Helen had been surprisingly gracious when Julie had given her notice. She still wanted to work with kids, but realized she was burned out, and not as effective as she could be when counseling them.

She had enough money saved up to support herself for six months, and if she got into trouble she could always go back home.

She got out of the car and leaned against it, eyeing the harbor. No, she couldn't go back home, it wouldn't be fair to Morgan. She'd be a constant reminder of his failure. She wouldn't do that to him.

As she ambled toward the dock, Julie hoped she could muster the strength to be pleasant to her host. Some days she could barely bring herself to smile. There would be other tourists on board, so she shouldn't have to work too hard. She could just lean back, relax and enjoy the scenery.

While in town she'd start her Christmas shopping for Mom and Lana. Somehow Christmas didn't feel all that joyous this year without Morgan.

She approached the tour boat, the *Susanna*, decorated in Christmas red, green and white lights. A part of her wanted to turn and walk away, but she forged ahead. It would be good to distract herself, to think about something else for a while, something other than her broken heart.

"Hello?" she called out.

"Come on aboard," a male voice answered from the cabin below.

She carefully climbed over the edge and waited for her tour guide. As she glanced across the channel, she appreciated that the waters were calm today. She should be frightened of the water after what she'd been through, but she'd made a deal with herself that she wouldn't let the Dynacorp criminals ruin the things she'd previously loved: the water, sunrises...

Morgan. Ugh. How long would it take to get over this? To mend the hole in her heart?

"Jules?"

She spun around and gasped at the sight of Morgan, stepping out of the cabin.

"I'm that scary, huh?" he joked.

"You're here."

He took her hand and pulled her against his chest. "Sweetheart, I'll be wherever you are. Always."

She clung to him for a second, then broke the embrace. "I don't understand."

"I'm an idiot. Sketch said so."

"I... But..."

"Shh." He pressed his forefinger to her lips and hugged her again.

"I heard you quit your job," he said. "What will you do?"

"Not sure yet."

"How about coming back to Port Whisper and helping them start up Horizon Farms?"

"You heard Joe offered me a job?"

"I did, and that you turned him down."

She looked into his eyes. "I thought every time you'd see me you'd be reminded of what you perceived as your own failure."

"Yeah, Sketch pointed out that's a little narcissistic on my part." He led her into the enclosed section of the boat and motioned for her to sit down.

"Where is everybody?" she asked, looking around.

"It's just us. Your sister set it up."

"Figures." She smiled.

Morgan shifted beside her and pulled a box out of his pocket. "I have an early Christmas present for you."

Still in shock, she couldn't speak. She opened the box. A beautiful silver locket in the shape of the sun shined back at her.

"I… It's beautiful."

"To remind you of the sunrise. I was going

to get you something else, but didn't want to be presumptuous."

"You mean…?"

"It's time to finally embrace the plan God has for us—to be together."

He leaned forward and kissed her. Her body flooded with love and her eyes welled with tears of joy. After a few seconds he broke the kiss and whispered in her ear.

"I love you, Jules. Always have, always will."

\* \* \* \* \*

Dear Reader,

How many of us have made a decision in our lives that seemed like a good one at the time, but as the years passed we wondered if it had been the right one? Living with regret can be frustrating and can hold us back from reaching our full potential.

Julie's story is about making a decision based on guilt, and discovering the beauty of self-forgiveness. It's also about believing in the grace of God, and opening your heart to His love.

This book holds a special place in my heart since it's about putting the past where it belongs—in the past—and embracing the possibilities and the wonders of love, friendship and God. As Julie and her high-school sweetheart, Morgan, evade danger, they make peace with their past and learn that through forgiveness anything is possible.

Thanks for giving me the chance to share this story with you.

Blessings,
*Hope White*

## Questions for Discussion

1. Did you agree with Julie's decision to flee danger by running back to Port Whisper? Why or why not?

2. Did you respect Julie for leaving her high-school sweetheart to pursue a career counseling runaways? Why or why not?

3. Have you ever known someone who carried the guilt burden? If so, how did you help open her/his heart to self-forgiveness?

4. Regarding Sketch, what do you think is the best way to help a troubled teen?

5. Have you known someone who had difficulty taking help from friends? If so, how did you get through to her/him?

6. Have you known someone who had a tendency to bury himself or herself in work? Why do you think this is?

7. Do you think Julie moved to the city out of guilt (because she couldn't save her friend) or because she wanted to help teenagers? Or was it a combination of both?

8. Have you known someone who, in their effort to help others, got into trouble themselves? How did they reconcile their efforts?

9. Do you think Julie was selfish when she left Port Whisper after high school? Why or why not?

10. Did you feel that Morgan and his father were at peace in this story? Why or why not?

11. Should Morgan have worked through his heartbreak and totally given up on Julie?

12. Was Morgan's resentment of Julie in the first part of the book justified?

13. Did you feel hopeful that Morgan would be able to help Sketch find his way?

14. Did you understand Julie's desire to leave Port Whisper—and Morgan—at the end of the story? Do you think it was a selfish or selfless decision?

# REQUEST YOUR FREE BOOKS!
## 2 FREE RIVETING INSPIRATIONAL NOVELS
## PLUS 2 FREE MYSTERY GIFTS

Love Inspired®
# SUSPENSE
### RIVETING INSPIRATIONAL ROMANCE

**YES!** Please send me 2 FREE Love Inspired® Suspense novels and my 2 FREE mystery gifts (gifts are worth about $10). After receiving them, if I don't wish to receive any more books, I can return the shipping statement marked "cancel." If I don't cancel, I will receive 4 brand-new novels every month and be billed just $4.99 per book in the U.S. or $5.49 per book in Canada. That's a savings of at least 17% off the cover price. It's quite a bargain! Shipping and handling is just 50¢ per book in the U.S. and 75¢ per book in Canada.* I understand that accepting the 2 free books and gifts places me under no obligation to buy anything. I can always return a shipment and cancel at any time. Even if I never buy another book, the two free books and gifts are mine to keep forever.

123/323 IDN GH5Z

Name _____ (PLEASE PRINT)

Address _____ Apt. #

City _____ State/Prov. _____ Zip/Postal Code

Signature (if under 18, a parent or guardian must sign)

Mail to the **Reader Service:**
**IN U.S.A.:** P.O. Box 1867, Buffalo, NY 14240-1867
**IN CANADA:** P.O. Box 609, Fort Erie, Ontario L2A 5X3

**Are you a current subscriber to Love Inspired® Suspense books
and want to receive the larger-print edition?
Call 1-800-873-8635 or visit www.ReaderService.com.**

* Terms and prices subject to change without notice. Prices do not include applicable taxes. Sales tax applicable in N.Y. Canadian residents will be charged applicable taxes. Offer not valid in Quebec. This offer is limited to one order per household. Not valid for current subscribers to Love Inspired Suspense books. All orders subject to credit approval. Credit or debit balances in a customer's account(s) may be offset by any other outstanding balance owed by or to the customer. Please allow 4 to 6 weeks for delivery. Offer available while quantities last.

**Your Privacy**—The Reader Service is committed to protecting your privacy. Our Privacy Policy is available online at www.ReaderService.com or upon request from the Reader Service.
We make a portion of our mailing list available to reputable third parties that offer products we believe may interest you. If you prefer that we not exchange your name with third parties, or if you wish to clarify or modify your communication preferences, please visit us at www.ReaderService.com/consumerschoice or write to us at Reader Service Preference Service, P.O. Box 9062, Buffalo, NY 14240-9062. Include your complete name and address.

# REQUEST YOUR FREE BOOKS!

## 2 FREE INSPIRATIONAL NOVELS
## PLUS 2 *FREE* MYSTERY GIFTS

*Love Inspired®* HISTORICAL

# READERSERVICE.COM

## Manage your account online!

- Review your order history
- Manage your payments
- Update your address

> *We've designed the*
> *Reader Service website*
> *just for you.*

## Enjoy all the features!

- Discover new series available to you, and read excerpts from any series.
- Respond to mailings and special monthly offers.
- Connect with favorite authors at the blog.
- Browse the Bonus Bucks catalog and online-only exculsives.
- Share your feedback.

*Visit us at:*
## ReaderService.com

RS15

# REQUEST YOUR FREE BOOKS!

## 2 FREE INSPIRATIONAL NOVELS
## PLUS 2
## FREE
## MYSTERY GIFTS

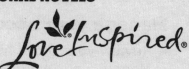

**YES!** Please send me 2 FREE Love Inspired® novels and my 2 FREE mystery gifts (gifts are worth about $10). After receiving them, if I don't wish to receive any more books, I can return the shipping statement marked "cancel." If I don't cancel, I will receive 6 brand-new novels every month and be billed just $4.99 per book in the U.S. or $5.49 per book in Canada. That's a saving of at least 17% off the cover price. It's quite a bargain! Shipping and handling is just 50¢ per book in the U.S. and 75¢ per book in Canada.* I understand that accepting the 2 free books and gifts places me under no obligation to buy anything. I can always return a shipment and cancel at any time. Even if I never buy another book, the two free books and gifts are mine to keep forever.

105/305 IDN GH5P

| | |
|---|---|
| Name | (PLEASE PRINT) |
| Address | Apt. # |
| City | State/Prov. | Zip/Postal Code |

Signature (if under 18, a parent or guardian must sign)

Mail to the **Reader Service:**
**IN U.S.A.:** P.O. Box 1867, Buffalo, NY  14240-1867
**IN CANADA:** P.O. Box 609, Fort Erie, Ontario  L2A 5X3

**Are you a subscriber to Love Inspired® books
and want to receive the larger-print edition?
Call 1-800-873-8635 or visit www.ReaderService.com.**

* Terms and prices subject to change without notice. Prices do not include applicable taxes. Sales tax applicable in N.Y. Canadian residents will be charged applicable taxes. Offer not valid in Quebec. This offer is limited to one order per household. Not valid for current subscribers to Love Inspired books. All orders subject to credit approval. Credit or debit balances in a customer's account(s) may be offset by any other outstanding balance owed by or to the customer. Please allow 4 to 6 weeks for delivery. Offer available while quantities last.

**Your Privacy**—The Reader Service is committed to protecting your privacy. Our Privacy Policy is available online at www.ReaderService.com or upon request from the Reader Service.

We make a portion of our mailing list available to reputable third parties that offer products we believe may interest you. If you prefer that we not exchange your name with third parties, or if you wish to clarify or modify your communication preferences, please visit us at www.ReaderService.com/consumerschoice or write to us at Reader Service Preference Service, P.O. Box 9062, Buffalo, NY 14240-9062. Include your complete name and address.

LI15